HEART OF HOPE

A SMALL TOWN ROMANCE

LUCY SCORE

ISBN: 978-1-945631-26-9 (ebook)
ISBN: 978-1-7282-8275-6 (paperback)

Published by Bloom Books, an imprint of Sourcebooks
P.O. Box 4410, Naperville, Illinois 60567-4410
(630) 961-3900
sourcebooks.com

lucyscore.com

070622

To Aunt Colleen for advising me to quit wasting my time writing Christmas letters and start writing novels.

PROLOGUE

*T*he fluorescent light above the hard vinyl bench where Bristol Quinn sat buzzed like a determined insect against a window screen. The doctor was still talking, but all Bristol could hear was the buzz.

Her sister was dead. *Buzz.*

"Head trauma... damage too extensive." *Buzz. Buzz.*

"Nothing more we can do." *Buzz.*

She heard her mother's stifled sob and mechanically wrapped an arm around the woman's waist. Her father's strong arm already rested on her shoulders like a lifeline. Together they would keep her anchored to this world. Bristol's older sister, Savannah, stood next to her, shaking her head from side to side as she tried to simultaneously process and reject the news.

"I'm very sorry," the doctor said, sinking down in front of them. "And I know this is a very difficult thing to hear, but Hope could still save a lot of lives."

Her little sister was the youngest EMT in Hope Falls history and had been studying to become a trauma surgeon.

The young woman who had more life in her eyes than most people did in their entire bodies was gone. It wasn't possible.

Bristol cleared her throat. The words came out in a stranger's voice. "You're talking about organ donation?" she asked.

He had tired, sad eyes nearly the same shade of gray as the hair that peeked out from under the green of his scrub cap. Bristol wondered how many times he'd had this conversation in the course of his career. Could someone ever become insulated, if not immune, from tiptoeing into the lives of families only to destroy the reality they'd held so dear?

How was she going to tell Violet that her beloved aunt, the woman who had helped raise her, was gone? Bristol shuddered at the thought. As her mother, it was her job to protect Violet. But there would be no softening this blow for either of them.

He nodded. "I know this is a difficult request to consider, especially at a devastating time like this. But we only have a small window of time."

Bristol forced herself to look at her father. Big Bob Quinn was a man of few words and a spine of iron. His normally smiling face was now uplifted toward the buzzing light, his broad shoulders shaking as a silent pain wracked his body. His eyes closed, and his lips were moving as if begging to wake up from a nightmare. Her mother, Mary, with her dark chestnut hair and Italian olive skin, leaned unblinkingly against her husband of thirty-one years. Savannah, the oldest of the Quinn girls, clutched the hand of her fiancé, Vincent. Her hazel eyes were red with tears that threatened to never stop flowing.

No one spoke.

"I think we should do it," Bristol said, mustering up a confidence that she didn't quite feel yet.

"I just don't know," Mary said, her voice as tight and frayed as an old thread. "I don't know."

Bristol squeezed her mother around the waist. "Mom, Hope would have wanted this. It's who she is." Her voice broke. She wasn't ready to change the tense of her little sister's life.

Savannah nodded. "We should do it," she echoed. "It's the right thing."

The doctor, whose name Bristol had forgotten the moment he'd spoken it, looked down at his hands. "I met Hope when she started her residency here. She was a very bright star in the emergency department."

Mary nodded, her mouth pinched in a tight line as if to hold back the wave of grief that threatened to overtake her. "Please donate her organs. It's what she would want."

Bristol's father reached out and put a large hand on the doctor's arm. "Please make her matter. Make this mean something."

"Mr. Quinn, I promise that this is the right decision. You will never regret this choice, and countless families will be grateful to you and your family for life."

~

Eight months later...

Dear Hope's Heart Recipient,

What a strange way to address a letter, but I don't have a name to go with the person who now has my sister's heart. In a way, besides our entire town stepping in to help us honor Hope's life, the biggest comfort my family has had in the past several months is the knowledge that our Hope lives on in you and the other recipients.

But this isn't a sad letter. I'm going to ask you for a favor, and I don't want to guilt you into it. Now, back to buttering you up.

My name is Bristol. I'm Hope's sister, and I hope that your recovery is going well. I thought maybe you'd like to know a bit about the woman whose heart you received because, frankly, she was pretty awesome. Hope was in medical school and planning to become a trauma surgeon, which pretty much put the rest of the family to shame for our career choices. I basically serve coffee for a living, and my older sister is an attorney who specializes in divorce, but Hope has been saving lives since she became an EMT at eighteen.

Of course, that's not the whole picture. She loved cats, the fatter the better. She hated sweet potatoes with a passion. She had zero interest in fashion and makeup, which the rest of the family joked was her primary reason for wanting to be a doctor. She owned more sets of scrubs than t-shirts. Hope loved slapstick comedy, and she snorted when she laughed. She loved to sing, even though she had the opposite of talent. She didn't have much time to read or watch TV, but when she did find the time, she preferred scary books and shows and then slept with the lights on.

Her favorite food was chocolate anything, and when she was a little girl, she wanted to be a garbage man when she grew up. She took ballet until she broke out in a spontaneous breakdancing routine in the middle of a recital when she was seven. She made the best pecan pie the world has ever known, and she once fell down the stairs running away from a bird that hopped through an open window in our parents' house.

So the reason I'm writing is two-fold. I thought you might like to know something about your new heart, and I'm back to that favor.

My older sister is getting married between Thanksgiving and Christmas. She considered postponing it, but to be honest, our family could use a shot of happiness. It would mean the world to all of us if you would consider attending the wedding. The ceremony will take place at Hope Falls Community Church at 4 p.m. on December 15, and the reception will be a huge party afterwards at Mountain Ridge Convention Center.

I hope you'll consider joining us. Meeting you and knowing that our sister lives on through you would be the best Christmas present I could ask for. But no pressure. Okay, maybe a little bit of pressure. Just kidding. If I don't hear back from you, I completely understand. There's something to be said for only looking forward in life, and I hope that your future is full of love, happiness, and all good things.

Hopefully yours,
Bristol Quinn

P.S. If you develop a sudden craving for putting ruffled potato chips on your peanut butter and jelly sandwich, that's all Hope.

1

Bristol was already awake and staring at the clock on her nightstand when the alarm sounded. She'd always been a morning person, but she found herself sleeping even less ever since... since.

She afforded herself one long, full-body stretch before putting her feet on the floor and officially starting her day.

She didn't bother reaching for any light switches as she tiptoed down the hallway until she hit the wide-open living space. Her daughter, Violet, took after Bristol's ex-husband and preferred late nights to early mornings. Bristol did her best not to wake the cranky, eight-year-old beast until absolutely necessary in the mornings.

She brewed a cup of coffee and took it to her favorite spot in the sprawling apartment. She'd had the contractor add a window seat to the rounded brick turret that overlooked Hope Falls' Main Street. It was the perfect vantage point for watching the small town hustle and bustle below. Still shrouded in darkness, Hope Falls slept peacefully. But the MMA gym across the street would be opening in an hour for the first round of classes, and downstairs Early Bird would be bustling with the morning breakfast crowd of athletes, fire-fighters, and high school students and faculty desperate for caffeine and protein.

Bristol had opened the trendy breakfast spot three years ago and never regretted it for a second. She'd bought the building, then a crumbling three-story pile of bricks, with help from her parents and her ex, Nolan, and turned it into a space where she could live and work. Close to her family and Violet's school and ideally located for the restaurant she'd planned for since college, it had felt like a dream come true.

She'd turned the retail space into a hip and homey spot to grab contemporary spins on traditional breakfast foods and coffees. Upstairs, she'd continued her renovation, leaving the exposed brick and ducting and designing a loft-style apartment around the tall, arching windows that overlooked Main Street and the fire station.

It was a large and airy space, and when her younger sister, Hope, had moved into her spare room during medical school, Bristol had felt like it really was home. Until it wasn't.

Hope's accident... *her death*, Bristol corrected herself, had ripped normal and happy away from all of them. In the days after Hope's funeral, Bristol had cleaned out her sister's room, packed away her things, and then had shut the door. That was eight months ago. Neither she, nor Violet, could bring themselves to open it again.

Enough reverie for the morning, Bristol chided herself. Life went on, even if she didn't want it to. She had a restaurant to open, a daughter to raise, and another day to get through.

She padded away from the window and into the kitchen. Turning on the lights that hung over the island, Bristol flooded the room with a soft glow. With her second cup of coffee, Bristol opened her laptop on the island and ran through her to-do list. Today was Saturday, which meant order day for the restaurant, and Vi had another hockey game in the afternoon. She made a mental note to dress warm. Not only had the cold snap arrived early in Hope Falls, but it had decided to stay. King's Pond was already frozen solid, and it wasn't much warmer inside the Kirkwood Ice Arena where the watered down hot chocolate served at the rink's dingy snack stand only did so much to keep parents warm.

She grimaced at the calendar. Thanksgiving was less than a week away, and Savannah and Vincent's wedding three weeks. It had been a hard year, and Bristol couldn't imagine the effort it would take for the Quinns to face the holidays and the wedding with smiles on their faces. Their first Thanksgiving without Hope. Bristol added a new item to her to do list: *Find Hope's recipe for pecan pie.*

If her sister couldn't be there with them, at least her Hope Falls Christmas Eve Carnival-winning recipe could be. A glance at the clock told her she'd dallied long enough. It was time to open up downstairs.

BRISTOL WAS STILL PULLING her long brown hair into a high ponytail when she pushed through the downstairs door of Early Bird. The convenience of her commute never lost its charm. One flight of stairs, and she was at work while Violet savored every last second of sleep before school.

Margo, part short order cook, part sous chef, was already there, turning on exhaust fans and starting the first pots of coffee of the day. She was a short, solidly built woman with red hair and cheeks. There was nothing traditionally beautiful about her, but Margo still managed to catch the eye of every man over fifty in town.

"Morning, Margo," Bristol said in greeting, rolling up her

sleeves and reaching up to flick on warming lights near the register. She'd designed Early Bird so she wouldn't need servers. Customers ordered at the register, and Margo or Bristol or whoever else was manning the beverage station called out names when orders were up. It was an efficient solution to quickly serve both eat-in and to-go customers. The standing queue for those waiting for to-go orders was organized around the community bulletin board that educated customers on everything from Hope Falls events to free kittens to music lessons.

The sit-down portion of the restaurant consisted of wooden tables in varying shapes and sizes surrounded by brightly painted contemporary metal chairs. The original floors, scarred from decades of use, had been sanded down and refinished to their current glossy glory. Shelves held tempting treats and gift ideas as well as books that spilled over from Read Between the Lines two blocks over. The brick walls served as gallery space for local artists. This month, Early Bird was featuring Tessa Maguire's landscape collection and nearly every one of the photographs had sold already.

"Still not sleeping, huh?" Margo asked as she inventoried the eggs and milk in the cooler.

"I sleep just fine," Bristol insisted.

"That why you're wearing two different sneakers?"

Crap. Bristol glanced down at her shoes, one gray and one navy. "You may have a small, tiny, practically miniscule point," she admitted.

Margo grunted and shook her head. She knew better than to try to talk Bristol into anything, especially taking a day off or coming in late.

"You're going to work yourself into spinsterhood if you don't start thinking about yourself for a change," the cook warned, shaking a metal spatula at her.

Bristol rolled her eyes and busied herself with the register, the espresso machine, and the smoothie ingredients. Spinsterhood, or its opposite, was not on her radar at this point. She'd tried marriage—very briefly—and hadn't liked it. Her relationship with Nolan had improved drastically as soon as the ink had dried on their divorce papers six years ago.

Since then, she'd managed the occasional date, but nothing serious ever materialized. Or, more accurately, she hadn't pursued anything serious. She had a daughter and a business. And now?

Now, she had a hole in her heart that no man or similar distraction could fill.

"How are Vanna's wedding plans coming?" Margo called from the depths of the kitchen.

"Good," Bristol yelled back. "Had our dress fittings a couple of days ago, and the good news is none of us gained forty pounds and ripped out the seams." Dress day had been an emotional one. Hope had been there the day Savannah chose her wedding dress, and they'd settled on the bridesmaid dresses. In fact, it had been Hope who encouraged Savannah to try on the fussy lace gown with the beaded bodice. And Savannah, the coolly logical woman who weighed all of life's big decisions with a detailed pro and con list, burst into tears when she saw herself in the dress.

There'd been tears again this weekend, but of a different kind. Hope's dress was there hanging on a hanger with no one to claim it.

The generally stoic Savannah had tearfully confessed in a dressing room that she didn't want to get married without Hope there. She'd hoped that a happy occasion would help the family heal. But now she was worried that what was supposed to be the happiest day of her life would end up being a painful reminder to everyone who was missing Hope.

"Do you still like your dress?" Margo asked, bustling in with a huge mixing bowl of sourdough pancake batter tucked under her arm.

Bristol nodded and bit her lip. "I did something probably really stupid," she confessed.

"Oh, Lord. You didn't change your mind and go with that tangerine sequined prom number did you?" Margo asked, mixing rhythmically.

"Oh, this is way worse," Bristol warned her. "Vanna was feeling pretty down about Hope after the fitting, so I went home and wrote a letter."

"To who? Hope?" Margo frowned.

"To the organ donation program at the hospital."

"Uh-huh," Margo said warily.

"The program is anonymous. So recipients don't know who donated and vice versa," Bristol explained. "But they allow both parties to write letters, if they so choose."

"And you so chose?"

Bristol nodded. "I wrote a letter to her heart recipient, and I..." she started to lose courage and trailed off.

"Oh, boy."

"Yeah. I invited the recipient to the wedding."

Margo stopped mixing.

"Did I make a huge mistake?" she asked.

Margo began to mix again. "The way I see it is there's three outcomes. One, you hear back from the recipient and they're a horrible human being, and your family is devastated. Two, the recipient is amazing, and your family finally gets some peace. Or, three, you don't hear anything from anyone."

"Well, let's hope it's not option number one," Bristol said dryly.

Margo patted her arm. "Honey, I think it was a beautiful sentiment and could do you all a lot of good."

"Thanks, Margo," Bristol said, feeling relieved.

"On the other hand, Hope's heart could be beating in some mafia hitman's chest as he rots in prison and passes the time selling drugs to other inmates."

"Thanks, Margo," Bristol groaned.

"I'm just messin' with you, honey. It's Hope's heart. Of course it went to someone who deserved it," Margo said with a conviction Bristol wished she felt.

There was a knock at the glass door, and Bristol waved a hand at the duo on the other side as she tied on her apron. "Ready for chaos?" she asked Margo with a grin.

"Bring it."

They opened at six sharp and closed up at eleven every morning, seven days a week. The hours gave Bristol the flexibility to be there for Violet after school and in the evenings. Not that her workday was ever over in five hours. There was always paperwork, ordering, accounting, and a thousand other things to manage. But Bristol loved it.

She unlocked the door for Deanna and Eli, firefighters just coming off a call from the looks of their tired, dirty faces.

"Morning, guys," she said, waving them both in the direction of Margo's fresh coffee.

"Hey there, Bristol," Deanna greeted her with a tired smile. Her light brown hair was escaping from the low ponytail that had been tied hastily at some point during the night. She had a smudge of soot on her chin.

"There's a face worth being awake for at this ungodly hour," Eli said with a wink. He breezed in just under six feet with dirty blond hair and a crooked grin that had the female out-of-towners blushing until closing at JT's Roadhouse. He was an incurable flirt, but beneath his charming exterior was a really nice guy who'd shoveled Early Bird's walk every snowfall since Hope died.

Both carried the acrid smell of smoke with them.

"How was the call?" Bristol asked.

"Car fire out on the highway," Deanna yawned and stretched her arms overhead. "No injuries, thankfully. But there's no way I'm dragging my ass to Lucky's class this morning. I need to fuel my body with something cheesy and carby."

"I think we can hook you up," Bristol said with a grin.

Bristol hustled back behind the counter and prepared for war as two more customers wandered in. Hope Falls may have been limited when it came to nightlife, but it sure put on a show for the early morning crowd.

She and Margo were Early Bird's only full-time staff. They filled in the schedule with a handful of solid part-timers who kept the place running at its highest efficiency. By seven every weekday morning, they found themselves running at full speed and stayed that way until nine or ten. Brunch on Sundays was growing steadily, and Bristol had been toying with the idea of adding another cook. But, as with every other decision this year, she'd found herself unable to pull the trigger.

Her world had been shaken, and there was no bouncing back from it. She was still just hanging on. Maybe someday she'd find that energy and drive that had her staring at a dusty pile of bricks and seeing a thriving enterprise, a happy home.

But for now, she'd hang on by her fingernails and hope for the best.

2

———

"**G**ood job, Vi!" Bristol shouted through her gloved hands as the little blur in purple skates hurried after the puck on the rink.

"Was that good?" Bristol's mother, Mary, asked next to her. The woman was wrapped under a blanket and enjoying a thermos of coffee rather than braving the Kirkwood Ice Arena's subpar hot chocolate.

"I have no idea," Bristol shrugged. "If she would have picked basketball or gymnastics, I'd at least have some idea of what's going on. And we'd be indoors."

She glanced around at the other fans crowding onto the metal bleachers and pulled her cheery red parka closer. The Hope Falls U-8 Polar Bears were battling the neighboring Longview Ice Picks in a dramatic match-up, at least according to the yells and stomps of the fans. Personally, Bristol thought people were cheering just to keep warm. Even with her limited knowledge of the sport, she knew the Polar Bears were terrible. But it was the first thing Violet had shown any interest in since Hope's death, and she was willing to do whatever it took to encourage that interest.

A particularly rousing cheer went up from the bleachers as little Noah Barnes skirted around Violet with the puck.

"Did we score? What was that?" Bristol demanded, coming to her feet with the rest of the crowd.

"Woo!" Her father pumped a fist in the air. "Vi just smashed that kid into the boards, and Noah got the puck."

"Is that good?" Bristol gaped. Sure enough, little number thirteen with her pigtails was leisurely skating away from a kid struggling to regain his footing on the ice. "That's not allowed is it?"

Bob grinned. "Way to go, Vi!"

"Maybe beating other kids up will help pull her out of her funk?" Mary offered hopefully.

"Gee, thanks Mom. That's exactly what I need, Vi to start kicking kids' asses on the playground," Bristol protested, but she waved back when Violet skated by waving and grinning. Smiles had become a rare occurrence in their home, and Bristol vowed then and there to let her little girl smash as many kids into walls as she wanted if it meant she got to see that dimple appear.

The ref blew a whistle about something, and Bristol sat back down and scanned the crowd again. There were familiar faces everywhere. It's what happened in Hope Falls. Strangers were only strangers for the 4.2 seconds it took Sue Ann Perkins to wheedle their life stories out of them. And speaking of strangers, Bristol spotted one leaning against the boards lining the rink angled her way.

He was tall with a chest and shoulders that looked broad enough to bench press a small vehicle. His hair was neither dark nor light from what she could see under his cap, but his neatly trimmed beard was brown with hints of red. He was well prepared for the November weather in a gray wool coat and boots. And that face. It may have been the few drops of

Washoe blood in her that had her thinking it, but the man looked like a warrior.

He didn't look friendly. He looked... intense, Bristol decided. And hot. Really, really hot.

The action on the ice had started again, but the stranger was still looking in her direction.

"It looks like you have an admirer," her mother hissed making a show of nodding in the man's direction. Subtly was not in Mary Quinn's vocabulary.

Bristol felt the color rise on her cheeks. "He's looking at someone behind us," she insisted, dragging her gaze away from his face and back to the ice.

"Mmm-hmm," her mom placated. "You know you're going to have to eventually start dating and having a sex life again someday, right?"

"Mother!" Bristol clapped a gloved hand over her mom's laughing mouth.

"Stop picking on our daughter, Mary," Bob warned without taking his eyes off the ice.

Mary laughed, her eyes sparkling under the knit snowflake headband she wore over her forehead and ears. "He's still looking, and it's definitely at you."

But before Bristol could argue or, better yet, sneak another peek in the man's direction, Violet's coach stole her attention.

Freddy "Tubs" Nelson had earned his nickname with his decades-long dedication to all foods fried and all fats trans. He visited Early Bird twice a week for his classic bacon with a side of bacon breakfast.

And he was currently clutching his left arm and going gray in front of her. "Coach?" Bristol called out, already on her feet. But he didn't answer. He was too busy going down like a slowly deflating balloon in the Macy's Day Parade.

Bristol scrambled over the last two bleachers and jumped

into the team bench. He was all the way down on the cold concrete. She rolled Freddy onto his back. His eyes were closed, and his jaw was slack. She felt for a pulse then, remembering her gloves, yanked them off, and felt again.

"Call 9-1-1," she ordered without looking up. "Crap, crap, crap."

She brought up last year's CPR training in her mind. She loosened Freddy's coat and leaned in listening for breath. "No breath. No pulse," she muttered to no one. "Okay. We can do this, Freddy."

Bristol interlaced her fingers and positioned the heel of her bottom hand at the center of his chest. "Here we go," she whispered. "One, two, three..." She counted off each compression, pretending it was the rubbery dummy from the class Hope had dragged her to at the fire station.

"Come on, Bristol," Hope had urged. "Everyone needs to know how to do this."

Well, she was doing it, and Bristol prayed she was doing it right. "Twenty-eight, twenty-nine, thirty." She paused, checked for breath. Finding none, she tilted Fred's head back and breathed into his mouth. His chest rose, and she gave him another breath before returning to compressions.

She knew there were people gathered around her, but she couldn't tell who they were or what they were saying. Her parents would keep Violet safe and away from the scene, and she hoped the parents and fans would do the same for the rest of the kids.

Fifteen, sixteen, seventeen...

She soldiered on through compressions and breaths until her arms felt like they were coming out of their sockets and her lungs were screaming. "How much longer for the ambulance?" she gritted out.

"Seven minutes," a chorus of worried voices responded.

Seven minutes? Hell, she and Freddy would both be dead by then.

It was on her fourth round of compressions that a pair of boots entered her field of vision followed by a portable AED defibrillator.

"Twenty-nine, thirty."

As soon as her hands left Freddy's chest, someone else's were yanking open his shirt. It was the stranger, she noted, as she took advantage of the break to wrestle out of her coat. A half-dozen hands behind her freed her from it, and she felt the winter air immediately cool the sweat that ran like a waterfall down her back.

"Check him for breath," the man ordered, his deep voice gruff but calm with authority.

She leaned in and then shook her head. "Still nothing."

The man quickly readied the AED. "I'm going to give him a shock, and then we're going to check him, okay? If there's still nothing, we go back to compressions."

We. We. We. The word echoed in her head along with her pulse. It made them a team, and right now, she liked that.

"Yeah, okay," Bristol nodded and helped him attach the pads to Freddy's bare chest.

"Everybody clear," the man ordered. He hit the button.

It was only after another round of compressions and the second shock that Freddy took a gasping breath on his own and his heart kicked back to life.

A few seconds later, his watery brown eyes fluttered open. "Hey there, Bristol," he whispered, his voice a wheeze. "How's about some of that maple candied bacon tomorrow?"

"How about an egg white omelet with a spinach smoothie?" she countered with a relieved smile.

"Party pooper."

Bristol gratefully sank down on the frozen ground as the

EMTs hauled ass onto the scene. Her arms felt like over-cooked spaghetti, and she had one hell of a headache brewing.

She caught the sad smile of the older paramedic. Raoul had trained Hope when she'd volunteered the summer before college, and he'd been the one to certify Bristol in CPR. He crouched down in front of her. "You did good, Bristol. Real good. She'd be proud of you."

"Thanks, Raoul," she said weakly. "Is Fred going to be okay?"

"He wouldn't dare die on us after all that hard work you two did," Raoul said, winking at her.

It was only then that Bristol looked around for her partner in life saving, but he was nowhere to be seen in the mob of people.

"Mom!" Violet's voice held the edge of panic that all mothers hate to hear from their child. Her daughter was trying to peer over the wall of boards that surrounded the rink. "Mom!"

Bristol climbed to her feet with the aid of a few helpful hands that also shoved her back into her coat. "I'm right here. Everything's fine, Vi," she promised.

"Is Coach Tubs okay?" Violet demanded, her blue eyes wide with worry beneath the plastic cage of her helmet. "Mr. Luke says if we don't have a coach, we have to forfeit. And Noah says that means lose on purpose. And I think that sucks."

"Violet!"

"Stinks. Sorry. Whatever. Mom, we need a coach!"

Luke Reynolds, Hope Falls' second professional snow-boarder and volunteer Pee Wee hockey ref skated up to the boards next to Violet. "We're going to need an adult volunteer to step in or the team forfeits," he confirmed.

"Isn't that just making the situation even more traumatic for the kids?" Bristol asked. "Can't we just wrap it up now?"

Luke shook his head regretfully. "League rules. Either both teams have a coach, or it's a forfeit."

"Sam is going to kill you if she hears about this," Bristol said, referencing the holy hell Luke's wife and fellow professional snowboarder, Samantha Holt, would bring down on him for destroying the hopes of an entire hockey team of children.

"That's why I'm looking at you really hard right now with sad eyes so you'll volunteer," Luke said, showing off his matching dimples.

"Go, Polar Bears," Freddy wheezed from the gurney, his arm raised high. The kids on the rink cheered and slapped the ice with their sticks. The crowd erupted at the display of life.

Bristol looked around her and saw a sea of parents avoiding eye contact. One didn't live in Hope Falls without knowing that one would eventually be dragged unwillingly into some unfortunate community service. "Crap. Fine. I'll coach. But just for the rest of the game."

IT WAS A BLOOD BATH. Literally. One of her kids got a bloody nose, though Bristol suspected it was from picking, not pucking. She'd assumed the other team would go easy on them seeing as how the Polar Bears had watched their coach almost fade from existence, but no. The Longview Ice Picks had ice in their hearts and methodically picked apart what defense a bunch of six- to eight-year-olds could muster with a coach who didn't even know how long a game... match... rampage lasted.

One of the players on the Picks looked like he was thirteen. He was a full head and shoulders taller than all of the other kids, and she wondered if the parents over in Longview fed their little hockey brats steroids. Bristol clearly heard him taunt Violet as he plastered her into the boards in front of the team bench. "Your coach almost died! Ha!"

Little bastard.

Apparently there was no mercy rule in hockey. The Bears took a beating, 3 to 11 by the time the final buzzer mercifully sounded.

"That sucked, Mom," Violet grumbled as they shuffled through the gravel parking lot.

Bristol didn't even bother to correct her. It had sucked. "Yeah, but try not to use that language around Lissa, okay? She'll think I'm slacking in my mom duties," Bristol said, guiding her slump-shouldered eight-year-old toward her step-mother's SUV.

"What are we going to do? We need a coach, Mom."

"I'm sure someone will volunteer," she said, hoping it was true.

"Hey, ladies," Lissa Graber, the wife of Bristol's ex-husband, greeted them. Lissa was easily the coolest person Bristol knew, even if she was an accountant. She had a short cap of thick, black hair, heavy-lidded brown eyes, and flawless mocha skin tone. Her wardrobe was impeccable, her nails always painted, and her organizational skills were second to none.

She was the kind of woman who wore a matching bra and underwear set every day of her life, Bristol thought.

Nolan was a lucky man.

"Hey, Lissa. We lost," Violet said morosely as Bristol helped her into the backseat next to her half-sister, Lyric, in her car seat.

"I'm sorry I missed it, kiddo. Lyric's doctor appointment

ran long. But I'll make it up to you and make spaghetti for dinner."

Violet pumped her purple mitten in the air. "Yes!"

Bristol walked around to the other side of the vehicle to tickle Lyric's round little cheeks. She had dark, curling hair like her mom, but her gray eyes were all Nolan. Lyric giggled.

"You're welcome to join us," Lissa offered to Bristol. "You know we love when Auntie Bristol stops by."

"Thanks, but I've got to track down a new hockey coach," Bristol said wryly. "I'll explain later. Vi, be awesome and call if you can't find your math book at Dad's, okay?"

"Okay. Bye, Mom," Violet said, brightening with the news of dinner.

Bristol watched Lissa pull away and wished something as simple as spaghetti could pull her from her own sadness.

3

*B*ristol squinted up at the ghostly halos around the rink lights. Her breath rose in a frosty cloud. She was flat on her back on the ice. Again.

She'd spent the afternoon and early evening dialing every responsible adult in Hope Falls looking for a hockey coach. And after she'd struck out—or whatever the corresponding hockey analogy was—for the hundredth time, she started looking for a semi-responsible teenager.

But the answers all echoed each other as if each parent had been provided a standard excuse list. No one had the time, schedule freedom, or desire to take over while Coach Tubs recovered.

And that was how Bristol Quinn had become the Polar Bears' new coach. Now, all she had to do was learn to skate and coach. It was peewee hockey. *How hard could it be?*

She flopped over and pressed up onto her hands and knees. Old Man King had kindly agreed to leave the pond lights on for her so she could practice without humiliating herself in front of the entire town. That was pretty much a direct quote.

He'd shown her where the switch for the floodlights was and how to lock up the gate before shuffling off to Sue Ann's Café for his dinner. Bristol had spent the majority of the next thirty minutes flailing and falling and feeling increasingly stupid.

"Why couldn't she like basketball?" she groaned to the night sky.

"Because hockey is a much better sport," a very deep, very male voice announced from somewhere beyond her field of vision.

She froze. She'd heard that voice only once before, but it had certainly made an impression as did the man it came from. Bristol turned toward the voice, and her worst fears were confirmed. The gorgeous stranger from this afternoon was standing on the ice watching her with amusement.

She swore quietly when his well-worn skates glided into her line of sight. Strong hands gripped her under the arms, and she was suddenly standing again. It lasted nearly a full second before her traitorous blades slid out from under her. Bristol face-planted against the man's very broad chest, but his gloved hands held her upright.

She looked up and realized her mistake too late. He was looking down at her, his lips still holding that amused smirk. But his eyes held something deeper, darker. His beard was full yet neatly trimmed, and Bristol could see flecks of red mixed in with the brown. His face was a study of the modern warrior. Below his snug wool cap, she could just make out the edge of a scar that split his eyebrow. He had another smaller scar beneath his left eye. His nose had the slightest curve as if it had been broken. But rather than taking away from his attractiveness, it only gave him a more dangerous appeal.

He'd looked tall this afternoon, but it was hard to gauge the height difference, first from a distance and then from crouched positions over Freddy. But now, standing toe-to-toe, he had several inches on her five-foot-seven frame.

"Hi," Bristol said a bit breathlessly.

"Hi," he returned, and his eyes warmed a bit.

"I'm Bristol," she offered.

"Beau." He grinned then. "I'd shake your hand, Bristol, but I'm afraid if I let go of you, you'll fall again."

Bristol gave an embarrassed laugh. "A very astute observation. What brings you to Hope Falls, Beau?"

"What makes you so sure I'm new here?" he asked.

"If you'd been here longer than a day, you'd know why. And the 'why's' name is Sue Ann Perkins. She's slacking if she hasn't introduced herself and weaseled all of your life's secrets out of you."

A shadow passed through those green eyes. "I haven't had the pleasure yet. Have you lived here long?"

"All my life. My whole family is here." *Minus one*, she reminded herself. She looked down, afraid he'd see her sadness with those canny eyes.

"I'm just here on business," he said finally.

She looked up again, curious what kind of business a man built like Beau would be in. "At Mountain Ridge? The convention?" she asked.

"Uh. Yeah. Yes, the convention," he said.

"You're a yoga instructor?" she asked, incredulously.

"What?"

"The California State Yoga Association. It's their annual corporate retreat at the convention center. There's like two hundred of you in town."

"Of course it is," he murmured almost to himself. "Uh, yeah. I love yoga."

"I may be being incredibly judgmental right now, but you don't look like a yoga instructor," Bristol told him.

Beau smiled, and she felt goose bumps that had nothing to do with the cold crop up on her skin. "Would I be just as judgmental if I said you didn't look like an ice skater?" he asked.

"Hockey coach," she corrected. "And rather than judgmental, I'd label you quite astute."

"You're coaching hockey?" Beau was laughing now, a booming sound that carried over the ice and into the dark.

"I'm glad you find the plight of a perfect stranger so humorous," Bristol sniffed, wriggling out of his arms.

"We saved a life together today. I don't think we can label ourselves strangers."

Bristol's feet tried to fly out from under her again, and with a squeak, she grabbed onto Beau's forearms to steady herself. His wide palms closed around her waist. "Perfect acquaintances then. Either way, unless you're here to give me skating lessons, I'd appreciate it if you left me alone."

"I leave you alone, and someone will find you tomorrow morning with your very pretty, concussed head frozen to the pond."

"I'm not that bad," she frowned at him.

"My mistake. Please, don't let me stop your practice." Beau let go of her waist and effortlessly pushed himself backwards.

"Show off," Bristol muttered and made a slow, sloppy turn away from him. No need to give him a front row seat to her humiliation. She nearly lost her balance when she tried to shoot a dirty look over her shoulder but regained her footing.

His laugh, much softer this time, warmed her cheeks.

Bristol bit her lip. "I can feel you judging me!"

"Sorry," Beau laughed. And then all she heard was the clean slicing of his blades on the ice. She didn't have to turn around to know that he was showing off by skating well.

Maybe she should call it a night? Maybe tomorrow after Early Bird closed she could watch some YouTube tutorials on learning to skate? She had until Monday before the next practice. She had to get better before then, or she'd be coaching from a lawn chair on the ice.

As her thoughts moved away from her feet and toward tomorrow, she didn't feel her balance fleeing until she was falling. She braced for impact, but her butt never hit the ice.

Beau had glided up behind her to play the hero and catch her under the arms as she fell.

"Ugh. How did you get so good at this?" she demanded. "There's nothing natural about a human on ice skates."

"Lots of practice. Why do you want to be a hockey coach? Why not find something that you're…"

"Less horrible at?" Bristol huffed as he righted her.

"I was going to go with 'more comfortable with.'"

"I would love to. I would be thrilled to help coach basketball or chess or cheerleading. But no, my daughter wants hockey, and if their team doesn't field a coach, they're done for the rest of the season."

He opened his mouth, but she plowed on. "And, yes, I have asked every other able-bodied adult in Hope Falls to coach, and not a damn one of them was available or willing. So it falls on me, and this is the only thing Violet has showed any interest in since Hope died, so I'm going to make it happen if I have to duct tape a pillow to my ass and give up sleep to research how to coach hockey."

She stopped and clapped her gloved hands over her mouth, looking horrified. "I am so sorry. I don't know where that came from."

"Sounds like it had to get out." He was looking at her with interest instead of the pity she expected.

She covered her face with her hands, and her feet immediately slipped. Beau held her upright by the waist. "It's been a rough year. My sister died, and we're all still... coping. And I haven't been pushing Violet, but I was so happy to see her so excited over something. I thought I could give her this, and she... A few months ago, she'd asked to start spending more time with her dad during the week, and that was a whole different kind of devastation. I feel like I'm losing my family piece by—"

The words came faster and faster until they shut off abruptly like a faucet valve being turned. She felt herself turning a violent shade of hot pink. "And here I am having verbal diarrhea all over a stranger."

"Acquaintance," he corrected again. "I can teach you."

"Teach me what?"

He lifted a shoulder, still maintaining his grip on her waist. "Skating, for one, and I could throw in the basics of hockey, too."

"You know hockey?"

"Who doesn't? Present company excluded, of course."

"And you're just willing to teach me?"

"I have the knowledge. You have the need."

"And just what would these private skating slash hockey lessons cost me?" Bristol asked warily.

"How about breakfast?" he asked.

Her blue eyes turned to icy fire. "Listen buddy, I'm not the kind of girl who meets a guy and has a one night stand. I have a daughter. I'm sure you can find someone else who's interested in a temporary bed warmer—"

"When I said breakfast, I meant only breakfast," Beau cut in. "At Early Bird?"

"How do you know that's my place?" she asked with suspicion.

Beau shrugged. "I'm staying at Mountain Meadow B&B. Shelby told me that 'Bristol's Early Bird makes the best omelets in town.' I assumed there weren't too many Bristols in Hope Falls."

There was something a little off in his explanation. But it wouldn't be the first time that Shelby and Levi Dorsey graciously threw business her way. Besides, Bristol was desperate enough that she was willing to overlook that nagging doubt. She needed help, and she needed it fast.

"My apologies. I'm not used to very attractive acquaintances asking me for breakfast. So you can teach me to skate, but do you know anything about hockey?" she crossed her arms, her gloved fingers drumming away on her upper arms.

"I can teach you everything about hockey. Unless you mean field hockey, in which case you're out of luck." His green eyes sparkled with humor.

"How do I know you're not some homicidal maniac looking for your next victim?"

"You're from small town America. You probably don't even lock your front door. Besides, I'm too charming to be a homicidal maniac."

"Tell that to Ted Bundy's victims," Bristol reminded him.

He grinned. "If only your in-depth knowledge of serial killers somehow translated into skating skills. Looks like you're going to have to take a leap of faith."

Bristol took a deep breath and let it out in a silvery cloud. "Come in tomorrow for breakfast. On the house," she said finally.

BEAU CLIMBED the front steps of the Mountain Meadow B&B following the glow of the porch lights to the front doors. He wasn't sure what he felt at this point. He'd met his objective for his first day in Hope Falls: *Make contact with Bristol Quinn.* She was different than what he'd expected. Scrappier, funnier, and sadder. There was a pain that lurked just beneath the surface of her gorgeous face.

She seemed real, honest. The pain he'd seen from her didn't feel like some kind of show she was putting on for his benefit. This was the raw Bristol Quinn, and he liked her.

For a man who dated mostly from the stereotypical girl-next-door pool—blue-eyed blondes—Bristol's exotic face was a gut-punch of a surprise. Her high cheekbones said Native American, and the sexy tilt of her wide eyes said something exotic. Her hair was long and straight, a chocolaty brown that framed the ocean blue depths of her eyes. When those full lips smiled, a dimple winked into existence in her right cheek. He couldn't stop staring at her.

But he wasn't here to find Bristol Quinn attractive, Beau reminded himself. *He was here to find out who she was and what she wanted.*

He'd liked her. A lot. But he'd been lied to and taken advantage of before. People had used him to get what they wanted. He had to be absolutely sure who she was before he'd even consider moving forward.

"Hey there. Beau, right?" Levi Dorsey called from behind the front desk. Well over six feet tall with sleeve tattoos and messy hair, he didn't look like the typical B&B owner, but Levi's wife, Shelby, fit the bill with her friendly smile and easy manner.

"Yeah, hi," Beau returned the greeting. "You must be Mr. Shelby."

Levi grinned, taking more pride than offense. "I am."

Beau offered his hand, and Levi accepted with a strong grip.

"You finding everything around town okay so far?" he asked.

"Easier than Chicago. And the traffic's better, too," Beau quipped.

Levi grinned as he shut down the computer. "Good. There's a bunch of menus and restaurant suggestions in your room if you need dinner. I'm heading out for the night, but if you need anything just give us a ring, okay?"

"Will do," Beau said, turning toward the stairs. But he paused. "Hey, do you know Bristol Quinn?" he asked, skimming his hand over the back of his head.

Levi looked up from the screen. "Yeah, sure. Tall, built, mile-long dark hair?"

"That's her."

"Her daughter's on my little brother's hockey team. She owns Early Bird across from the fire station. Makes a hell of a breakfast, and that's coming from a B&B owner."

Beau had held off on asking Shelby about Bristol when he'd checked in earlier in the day. He'd been a lifelong Chicago native, but it didn't take more than thirty seconds of Shelby's "where are you from, and what brings you to town" interrogation to realize that small towns had few secrets. It would be better if no one knew why he was really here. But Levi here looked like he knew when and how to keep his mouth shut.

"That's high praise then. I, uh, met her this afternoon. She seemed... nice."

"She's single. If that's what you're wondering," Levi offered with a conspiratorial smile.

And that was a miscalculation. Small town gossiping wasn't limited to just those with estrogen, Beau realized.

4

*S*unday brunch at Early Bird meant stuffed French toast, an out-of-this-world eggs Benedict special, fluffy quiches and crepes, and piles and piles of bacon. It also meant large, hungry crowds. It was all hands on deck behind the counter and in the kitchen. Bristol liked to help out with the later morning crowd, but knowing that the mysterious Beau would be making an appearance had her showing her face as the open sign was flipped on.

"What are you doing here so early?" Margo demanded in lieu of a greeting.

Bristol nervously brushed her hair back from her face. "What? I thought I'd come in a little early today."

"You're wearing makeup." Edwin Ruiz was seventy-two years old and had worn bifocals for thirty of those years, but the weekend grill cook could see that she'd swiped on a coat of mascara. Okay, and maybe some subtle eye shadow. And foundation. And a sweep of lip gloss... over the lip liner.

"Hey, those are cute earrings," Maya Ruiz, Edwin's grand-daughter and Bristol's part-time barista, chirped as she breezed past, coffee pots in hand.

"So what's the special today?" Bristol asked, changing the subject. She made a personal note to actually attempt an effort when it came to her appearance from now on so people wouldn't read into a tinted ChapStick in the future.

"Hang on to your hats," Margo announced cheerfully. "It's tater tot casserole with maple candied bacon and gruyere cheese."

"It sounds like a heart attack on a plate," Bristol said.

"Speaking of heart attacks, when were you going to mention that you and some insanely hot stranger saved Tubs' life?" Margo shot back.

"Heard you gave him mouth to mouth," Edwin called, poking his head around the wall of the kitchen, his bushy white eyebrows wiggling like caterpillars. "Most action he's had in a decade."

"Very funny. Any of you gossip mongers hear how he's doing today?" Bristol asked, helping herself to a cup of coffee.

They filled her in on the latest, including Freddy's current vital signs that were so detailed Bristol was sure a HIPAA violation had taken place. "He's on the mend," Margo said with the confidence of a medical professional. "So who was your hunky sidekick?"

"Oh, look," Bristol said, nodding to the door. "Customers."

The early morning crowd was slower on Sundays, but word about Freddy's near death experience had clearly spread, and everyone wanted to get her firsthand account of it. Even Sue Ann Perkins, in her long skirt and matching purple sweater set, swung by on her way to church.

"I heard you're a real life hero," she said, wrapping her strong arms around Bristol and dragging her in for a hug.

Bristol shook her head. "I was just in the right place at the right time," she said, embarrassed. *Was this what Hope had felt every time someone recognized her for a good deed?* she wondered.

"Your sister would be really proud of you."

"I sure hope so," Bristol said, giving the woman an affectionate squeeze. She and her sisters had known Sue Ann their entire lives. On the day of Hope's funeral, Sue Ann had shut down her own café and showed up with her staff to open up Early Bird so all of Bristol's employees could attend the services. The woman's generosity still brought a lump to her throat.

"Now, before I forget, Kelly mentioned there was a man that stopped by the café yesterday asking where he could find you."

"Did she say who?" Bristol asked.

Sue Ann shrugged her shoulders. "Her exact words were a 'hot, hot, hot stranger.'"

Kelly King was a part-time server at Sue Ann's café and about as pleasant as a cactus. She had an eye for anything with a penis and considered every woman under fifty a competitor for said penises.

"Her description of him lined up with everyone else's description of the equally handsome stranger at the rink yesterday afternoon," Sue Ann continued.

Beau. He must have tried to find out who she was after he left the rink that afternoon. Maybe it wasn't a coincidence that he'd shown up at the pond during her pathetic night skate? She felt a little thrill run through her. Could Beau actually be interested in her? How long had it been since she'd been the object of interest or felt any interest herself?

"Honey?" Sue Ann was snapping her fingers in front of Bristol's face. "Where'd you go?"

"Sorry, Sue Ann. It must have been Beau. He's in town on business. We met when he helped with Freddy yesterday afternoon, and then we ran into each other again that evening."

"Hmm." Sue Ann looked as though she had a lot more to say on the subject, but the jingle of the front door bell interrupted her.

Beau walked in, looking just as good as he had yesterday. He took in the controlled chaos, the crowded tables, the shouts of orders up, and shrugged out of his grey wool coat. He wore jeans and a burgundy Henley that fit him like a second, well-toned skin.

"Well, that must be our mystery man," Sue Ann said, eyeing him up. Beau spotted Bristol then and smiled that heartbreaker grin. His eyes crinkled.

"Oh my." Sue Ann sighed turning back to Bristol, who was sure she'd just set her own hairline on fire with the blush that scorched her face.

He ambled over, moving with grace and power packed into every inch of his hard body. It did nothing to cool her cheeks.

"Morning, Bristol," he said.

"Hi, Beau," she said, wondering why her stomach was suddenly fluttering. Sue Ann stepped on her foot and smiled expectantly. "Oh! Uh, sorry. Beau, this is my friend Sue Ann Perkins. Sue Ann, this is Beau. He's in town for the yoga convention," Bristol said, hastily making the introductions.

Beau offered his hand to Sue Ann. "I've heard a lot about you," he said with a wink in Bristol's direction.

Sue Ann's laugh reverberated throughout the café. "Well, that puts you one up on me. I'll have to catch up. Where are you from?"

"Chicago," Beau answered, but he was looking at Bristol.

"Uh-huh. You have family there?" Sue Ann continued down the list of her questions. Bristol had heard the interrogation often enough that she knew the next six questions by heart. But judging from Beau's stricken expression, he wasn't prepared to play two hundred questions with Sue Ann.

She was wondering if she should step in and rescue him or not when Maya waved frantically from the counter and pointed to the register.

"If you two will excuse me, I have to fix something."

~

BEAU FELT something akin to panic climbing up his throat as he watched Bristol retreat behind the counter, leaving him with the town busybody. He'd been interviewed before, hundreds of times. But that was his past life, and he wasn't prepared to relive it at the hands of a nosey Sunday school teacher. He had an objective, and that objective wouldn't be met if his identity became public knowledge.

"Okay, she's gone now," Sue Ann announced. "Let's get down to business." She pulled him over to an empty two-top table by the coffee station and sat. Not knowing what else to do, Beau sat down across from her. She took a dainty sip of her coffee and eyed him up. "I'm going to guess that you're not in town for a convention."

Before he could argue or deny it or outright lie, she held up a hand. "I happen to know that you stopped in to my café yesterday morning to ask some questions about Bristol. And that was before you even met her."

He opened his mouth, but she shook her head at him. "I further know that you went to the arena looking for her that afternoon, *and* my dear friend Mr. King also reported seeing you in the parking lot that evening when Bristol was skating." The woman leaned in. "Now, you don't look like a serial killer to me, but you sure as heck aren't a yoga teacher either. So I've gotta ask you, do you mean Bristol any harm? Because I can start screaming bloody murder right now if you are."

What was it with this town and thinking every stranger was out to chop them up into pieces? Beau wondered.

He shook his head hard. "No, ma'am. I'm just here to make sure Bristol is... who I think she is."

Sue Ann narrowed her eyes and leaned in. "I have no idea what that means, but Bristol and the rest of the Quinns have been through the wringer this year. I won't stand for anyone trying to cause them any trouble."

Beau put his hands up in a gesture of peace. "I can't tell you what I'm doing here. But I promise you, Ms. Perkins, I won't cause Bristol any trouble."

Sue Ann nodded briskly and stabbed a finger at him. "I'll be watching you. You just remember that."

"Yes, ma'am. I appreciate that."

Satisfied, Sue Ann hopped out of her chair with the energy of a woman half her age. "Good. Now if you'll excuse me, I have to make my rounds before church." And with that, she left Beau to sag with relief into his chair.

It was barely seven o'clock in the morning, and he was already exhausted. His little mission was turning out to be more complicated than he'd thought it would be. He felt the weight of a gaze and looked up. Bristol was grinning at him from behind the counter. She crooked her finger at him, and he felt himself standing as if on autopilot.

At least Sue Ann hadn't sprinted up to the front of the line to warn her, Beau thought consoling himself.

"Are you ready to order now that your interrogation is over?" Bristol asked with a teasing smile.

She looked even prettier today than yesterday. Her hair was pulled back in a high ponytail, and under the pendant lights that hung above the counter he could pick out all the shades of blue in her eyes. She was wearing gray leggings and a black tunic top that dipped low in the back. The yellow apron with huge red flowers somehow made her even sexier.

"Does everyone in town have to face Sue Ann?" Beau asked, leaning over the glass display case that housed a circus of colorful pastries and baked goods.

Bristol nodded. "No one's a stranger for long in Hope Falls. Now, what can I get you for your complimentary breakfast?"

Beau read over the handwritten menu boards hanging on the wall behind her and whistled. It was quite the eclectic collection of breakfast foods. "I could use a recommendation."

"Healthy or artery clogging?" Bristol asked.

"Healthy, but I still want it to taste good."

"I find your lack of faith deeply offensive," she said, wrinkling her nose.

"My apologies. I'll bow to your expertise," he teased.

"One soy patty with tofu relish coming up," she quipped, her fingers flying over the screen. "To drink?"

"Coffee. And," he read over the juice list. "How about the Immunity Booster?"

"Good choice." Bristol handed him a mug and pointed him at a table. "Grab some coffee and have a seat. When you hear me yell your name that means your food is up."

"I don't suppose you could eat with me? I mean, so we can talk about your lessons." *He was researching*, he told himself. *Not flirting.* He needed to get to know her, and the only way he was going to do that was to spend time with her.

"I might be able to spare a few minutes," she said.

He spotted the dimple when it appeared next to her mouth and felt something warm spread through his gut. Okay so maybe he was flirting a little bit, but it couldn't do any harm. *Could it?*

"I'll save you a seat," he promised. He filled his mug with the French roast and settled back at the table Sue Ann had confiscated for their little chat. This time he didn't have anything distracting himself from the view.

Bristol moved with speed and efficiency, dancing around the younger barista with the hipster glasses and tiny nose stud while greeting customers by name. Her kitchen crew rotated out front sliding plates of hot food under the tiered heat lamps and shouting out names. No one waited more than a few minutes for their breakfast, and Beau was no different.

His meal, however, was delivered by the very attractive owner. Bristol slid his plate to him and handed over a glass of green juice that he eyed suspiciously. In training, he'd been known to down whatever concoction his nutritionist put in front of him. But now he had freedom of choice, and he enjoyed exercising it.

"Don't look at it like that," Bristol said, sensing his hesitation. "It tastes like apple juice, but if it's too scary for you, I can get you a juice box or a chocolate milk."

"You're pretty snarky for someone who depends on happy customers for her livelihood," he teased her, admiring the omelet artfully arranged on his plate.

"It's all part of my charm," she said airily, taking a sip of coffee. "So did you enjoy your chat with Sue Ann?"

"Did she, by chance, ever work professionally as an interrogator?" he asked, digging into the eggs.

"Maybe in a past life," Bristol laughed.

Beau took a forkful of omelet. "Oh, my God. This is good."

"Of course it is," Bristol said, rolling her eyes. "You don't have to act so surprised."

"Sorry, but I thought your mad skills on the ice could possibly translate to your culinary expertise, and everyone in town loved you so much they didn't want to hurt your feelings, so they just keep showing up every day and shoveling down terrible food."

She blinked. "Har har. I should have served you the tofu," she fired back, reaching for his plate.

He slapped her hand away. "Uh-uh. Mine. What's the spice in here?"

"Jalapeños. Try it with a bite of the beans on the side. Lots of protein, low fat, and pretty damn delicious."

"My compliments to the chefs."

The dimple was back when she wrapped her slim fingers around the snowflake mug of coffee she'd brought for herself. "So what time tonight?"

"Pick you up at seven?"

"I can just meet you at the pond," she said.

"Now who's being a baby? We're going to the same place at the same time."

"I'm not being a baby. I'm being a responsible adult. I don't know you. I don't even know your last name."

He glanced down at his coffee. "It's French." The lie rolled off his tongue awkwardly. He offered her his hand. "Beau French."

"Why is it I feel like everything you tell me isn't entirely accurate?" Bristol asked, grudgingly accepting his handshake.

"Beats me. Maybe the high crime rate and unusual number of grifters per capita in Hope Falls make you suspicious?"

"That must be it." She tugged her hand from his grasp.

"Look," Beau said, leaning forward. "Sue Ann already vetted me. I'm officially not a serial killer. I'm just offering you some pointers on skating... and hockey. And eating free breakfast."

"Okay, but if you try to murder me and dump my body in the woods, I'm going to be pretty pissed off."

"So noted."

5

———

"What's this about you and some hot guy named Beau saving lives and having breakfast together?"

"Well hello to you, too, Vanna," Bristol said dryly into her phone. She held up the sweater in front of her and frowned in the mirror.

"I'm serious. The entire town is talking about you. Your name came up in a staff meeting this morning," Savannah said.

Bristol tossed the sweater on top of the growing pile of discarded clothes on her bed. "You lawyers are so funny. Always cracking jokes."

"Swear to God," Savannah insisted. "I don't know if everyone's more excited about you saving Coach Tubs' life or having a hot guy chasing you around town."

"He's not chasing me," Bristol grumbled, reaching for a red turtleneck. "He just happened to be at Vi's game and basically saved Fred's life. Then I ran into him later that night when I was skating."

"Hold it. Why were you skating?" her sister demanded,

zeroing in on the answer like a trial lawyer picking apart witnesses.

"Oh, haven't you heard? I'm the Polar Bears' new hockey coach."

The peal of laughter on her sister's end had Bristol yanking the phone away from her ear and then pulling it back when she realized how long it had been since she'd heard Savannah laugh like that.

"I'm glad you find this so amusing," Bristol said dryly.

"You can't even skate. You don't even know what the penalty box is!"

"*I* know that! But every other parent on the team flat out refused to take over, and without a coach, their season would be over, and Vi would be devastated."

"Why can't Nolan coach her? He's Mr. Outdoorsy."

"No, he's Mr. Outdoorsy Sales Guy," Bristol corrected her. "There's a huge difference. Plus he's traveling a lot right now. He's hitting up a bunch of snowboarding competitions for work. Anyway, Beau is teaching me to skate and giving me some hockey pointers. I can do this. It's only until Christmas."

"Uh-huh. Well you can be sure that I'm coming to the next game."

"I'm going to pretend that you're showing up to support Violet, not laugh at me."

"I can multitask."

"Don't you have a wedding to plan?"

"I'm a Type A attorney. The wedding has been planned down to the napkin rings since about six seconds after Vince put a ring on it."

"You're such a hopeless romantic," Bristol teased.

"Stop deflecting. And tell me more about this Beau guy. Rumor has it he's gorgeous."

It had been a hundred years since she'd gossiped about boys with her sisters. She felt rusty but good.

"Let's just say the rumors, for once, aren't completely overblown. He's big. Tall, broad shoulders, muscles. And he has these bright green eyes that look like they're looking right into you. Did I mention he's got a beard?"

"He sounds very lumbersexual," Savannah sighed.

"I haven't seen him in a flannel yet. I honestly can't get a read on him. He's funny and smart. But every time I talk to him, I go into the conversation determined to find out more about him. And then I get dazzled by his smile or his butt, and I walk away with more questions than answers."

"If I weren't a cold-hearted bitch, I'd say you've got quite the crush."

"And since you are a cold-hearted bitch?"

"I'd say you're lusting after a hot guy. When's the last time you got laid?"

"Savannah Quinn!"

"What? Just because you're a mom doesn't mean you're not allowed to see any action. In fact, you should be contractually obligated to have hot sex every once in a while."

"I'm not a nun!" Though it had been a while... quite a while. "Quick question, totally unrelated. How long can you go without sex before you're a virgin again? Asking for a friend."

Savannah laughed again, and Bristol let the sound light up the dim corners of her heart.

"Take some advice from your legal counsel. Go get laid. Enjoy it. And then go back to momming and businessing."

"Does Vince know what a lucky man he is?" Bristol asked.

"I remind him a dozen times a day. Sooner or later it'll stick. But seriously, it's nice to see you feeling something."

"Back at you," Bristol sighed. The whole family had been

numb for so long, the past twenty-four hours had felt like a bit of a thaw. "It's nice to hear you laugh."

"Yeah, well. If we're not laughing, we're crying. And I'm sick of crying."

"Hey, do you want to come over and get super drunk on Black Friday?" Bristol asked. It had been their own holiday tradition since they were both of drinking age. Violet would be traveling with Nolan and Lissa to Lissa's parents' house for their family celebration, and without Hope, the apartment would feel too empty.

"That depends. Can we steal desserts out of Early Bird's bakery case and watch Christmas movies?" Savannah asked.

"Duh. It's tradition."

"Count me in."

The clock on her nightstand caught Bristol's eye. "Crap. I have to go. Beau's picking me up in ten, and I'm not dressed yet."

"Consider staying that way and forgoing the skating lessons," her sister suggested.

"How about I get to know him first and make sure he's not an insane axe murderer?"

Savannah sighed heavily. "Fine. Send me some proofs of life tonight so I can make sure you're not dead. Unless you're having sex. Don't send me any of those selfies."

THE ONLY ACKNOWLEDGEMENT of her sister's advice was the pretty bra Bristol hooked on under her sweater. She went with a black ribbed turtleneck and gray and black striped fleece leggings that made her butt look pretty damn great. She finished the look with a wool cap and a warm down-filled vest, both in fire engine red.

She'd touched up the morning's makeup and added a thick layer of lip-gloss to ward off the winter wind.

Her phone sounded an alert, and she saw a text from Beau.

I'm downstairs. Want me to come up?

She thought about her sister's suggestion for alternative evening plans, grabbed her bag, and sprinted for the stairs.

On my way down.

She'd never brought a man into the apartment she shared with her daughter. It seemed... weird. The men she had dated since her divorce had remained neatly compartmentalized in the tiny sliver of life she dedicated to her own free time. It was safer that way, less messy.

She pushed through the glass door next to Early Bird's entrance. Beau was leaning against a dark blue SUV, his hands shoved in the pockets of his heavy jacket. He was studying her with an unreadable look that had her slowing her approach.

"What?" She glanced down at her outfit, fearing that she'd forgotten to put on the pants she'd picked out.

"Nothing," he said, shaking his head. "Just... hi."

"Am I dressed okay?" she asked.

"You look great," he said. "I mean you look warm."

"Are you nervous?" she demanded, cocking her head to one side.

He scratched the back of his head with a gloved hand. "Of course not. What's to be nervous about?"

"Spending time alone with me in the dark. Maybe you're a vampire, and you won't be able to control your thirst for human blood?"

"So I'm now an undead murderer?"

At least he was smiling.

"The evening is young," Bristol shrugged. "I guess we'll find out."

He opened the passenger door for her and leaned in close when she slid onto the seat. "Good thing you wore a turtle-neck," he winked, flashing her his teeth.

Bristol was pleasantly surprised to find that her seat warmer was already on. *Funny, sexy, and thoughtful?* Maybe Savannah had the right idea after all. But as a respectable adult, Bristol had a responsibility to learn a few things about Mr. Beau French before she even considered taking his pants off.

6

*H*e spent the short drive to King's Pond skillfully evading Bristol's questions about his day at the yoga convention.

"Do you teach those hot power insane yoga classes? You know, the ones where they crank the heat up to like two hundred degrees?" she asked as he pulled into the gravel lot at the pond.

"Bikram?" he'd done some frantic internet searches the night before so he could at least drop some yoga vocabulary every once in a while to build up his cover story. "Have you ever taken one of those classes?" he asked, turning the tables on her.

Bristol shook her head, and the pom-pom on top of her hat swayed. "I like to think being on my feet next to heat lamps five hours a day is the equivalent."

"You're probably not wrong," he said, turning off the engine.

Bristol stared out her window at the rink. "I really wish Vi would have been into some other sport," she sighed morosely.

"Hockey is not that bad," Beau laughed.

"Ugh. I know. It's just she's really into it, and I want to support that. I haven't seen her show any interest in anything since..." Her words trailed off, and she shook her head. "Anyway, I just wish she could have chosen something that I at least remotely understood."

"It's not that complicated. I'll help you with the basics, and we'll go from there, okay?"

"Why *are* you helping me?" Bristol asked.

And just like that, the suspicion was back. He almost laughed.

"You're a nice girl doing a nice thing for her daughter. Plus, that breakfast this morning was amazing, and hockey is kind of my hobby."

"So it all works out?"

"If you do what I say, it will. But if you're stubborn and resist my genius teaching techniques, it'll be a disaster."

"I'm not stubborn!"

Beau grinned at her gasp of outrage. "I think you're used to doing things your way. But you're just going to have to trust me here."

They got out of the car with Bristol grumbling under her breath. He unloaded his skates and a box from the back of the SUV. When she started toward the rink's office he stopped her.

"Where are you going? The ice is this way."

"Mr. King lets me use the rental skates. I don't have my own," she explained.

Beau shook his head. "Those crappy rentals were probably half the reason you were falling down last night."

"What do you want me to do? Shuffle around in my boots?"

He guided her over to a bench next to the pond and gave her a little push to make her sit. "I want you to wear these." He pushed the box at her.

She raised a skeptical eyebrow but lifted the lid of the box as fast as a sugared up kid on Christmas. "Holy crap!"

"Do you like them?" He'd had to drive to Tahoe to a specialty shop to find the right ones. "I think half the reason you were falling all over yourself yesterday was the toe pick on the rental skates. These are hockey skates." He plucked one out of the box and held it up. "See? No toe pick."

"Beau," she looked up at him with those blue eyes warm and wide. "That was really sweet of you."

He shuffled his feet, feeling a little embarrassed and a lot guilty. "It's no problem. You'll have an easier time with these."

"What do I owe you?"

He was already shaking his head. "Nothing. They're a gift."

"That's not part of our deal," she reminded him. "I can't accept these. It's too much."

"Just try them out tonight, and if you're still being stupid and stubborn later, I'll take them back," he suggested, pulling her foot into his lap and yanking off her boot. He slid her socked foot into the skate and expertly laced it. His fingers seemed to have a mind of their own when they wrapped around her slim calf.

"They're warm," she exclaimed. "And they fit!"

"Thermal lining and I guessed," he told her, making quick work of her other foot before lowering her feet to the ice. "There."

Bristol sat admiring the grey and pink skates while he quickly laced his up. He rose and offered her his hands. "Ready?"

She took a deep breath and put her gloved hands in his. Biting her lip, she let him pull her to her feet. "Oh!" she said in surprise.

Beau grinned down at her. "More stable, aren't they?"

She looked up at him. "I don't feel like my ankles are going to shatter."

"Good. Okay, I'm going to pull you so you can get a feel for them. Ready?"

She nodded, and he smoothly skated backwards, towing her along with him. Her posture was tense, her grip on his hands tight.

"How do they feel?"

"Really good," she admitted.

"Good enough to keep?"

She started to make what Beau could only assume was a smart comment when her foot slipped. She yelped and gripped his hands harder.

"Good recovery," he told her. "Ready to try pushing off?"

"Don't let go!"

"I'm not letting go of you," he promised. "Here we go. Just shift your weight into one skate while you push off with the other. Careful—"

She didn't give herself a gentle nudge as he thought she would. No, Bristol shoved off and sent herself sprawling into his chest. He caught her with a laugh. "I take it patience isn't your strong suit?"

She wrinkled her nose. "I hate not being good at things."

"No one is good at skating right away."

"You're really good at it," she argued.

"Gorgeous, I've been skating since I was six years old. That's twenty-three years of experience."

"You're twenty-nine?" she asked with obvious pleasure. "Thank God. I was worried you might be younger than..." She trailed off and her cheeks burned pink.

"Thirty in a month. But what does that matter?" he teased. There was only one reason he could think of that a woman would care about his age. And he hated to admit it, but he liked that her mind was working in that direction.

"Well, I… uh… you know…" She was floundering like a fish out of water.

"Do I know?" he asked.

"Oh, shut up," Bristol muttered. "I haven't had a conversation with a man alone in I don't know how long."

"Is this a date?" Beau asked, suddenly fascinated by her embarrassment.

"No! Of course not!"

"Because if it was," he said, lowering his voice. "I'd make any excuse in the book to get closer to you." He reeled her in by the forearms. Eyes that had been glued to her feet met his gaze. She wet her lips, and he felt his breath catch in his throat.

Beau could dive into and drown in those blue depths if he wasn't careful. And that wasn't why he was here. But damn if he could pull away from her. She was beautiful, smart, and damned hilarious. He was attracted to her more than he'd been to any other woman in recent memory… hell, in any memory. When she smiled, his mouth curved up on the sides in an involuntary reaction. When she laughed, he felt a heat slide through him more potent than any skimpy outfit or bedroom-eyed puck bunny.

It wasn't just her looks because, hell, she was beautiful. Breathtaking, punch-in-the-gut gorgeous. It was what bloomed beneath that flawless skin and those sexy sweet eyes. She had attitude, strength, and a driving desire to do right by others. It was a potent combination, and Beau was afraid that he wouldn't recover from it if he got too close. He shouldn't be doing this.

"Bristol?" he said her name softly.

"Yeah?" She was breathless, looking up at him with those big eyes, her rosy lips parted.

"You're skating."

It took a second for the words to process. But when they did, he had the pleasure of watching her eyes light up.

"Oh my, God! Beau, I'm skating!"

He was still holding on to her arms, but Bristol was gliding on her own, one foot at a time.

"Want me to let go?" he offered.

"No! I mean... not yet."

~

"YOU'RE A GREAT COACH," Bristol said for the third time as Beau slid into the driver seat.

"You're an excellent student," he told her.

Bristol preened a bit. She had kicked ass on the ice tonight. It was a complete one-eighty from her experience the night before. Sure, she'd fallen a few times, but under Beau's patient tutelage, she'd progressed to slowly skating the length of the rink under her own power several times.

He'd given her tips and guided her into a more natural stance. And it had worked. Now if she could just learn all the finer points of the sport, she'd be set for Wednesday's game.

"What are you doing out here in the dark teaching a stranger to skate?" Bristol asked, studying him in the dome light.

"I'm just getting to know you," he said.

"But why? Why me?"

"Why not you? You're smart, you're the most beautiful woman I've ever seen, and you serve up a hell of an omelet. What's not to find intriguing?"

"Intriguing? I've never heard that word applied to me before." Reliable, yes. Consistent, of course. But intriguing?

"Is that one of the hazards of growing up in a small town? When everyone's known you since you were three so no one actually sees you."

"That's an oddly astute observation," Bristol admitted. "We've all known each other for a hundred years, so it's practically impossible to take a step back and see someone with fresh eyes."

Beau guided the SUV toward the road leading back to town. "What about your family? What do they see when they look at you?"

Bristol shook her head. "I honestly don't know. We've gone through a rough time this year. I know I blurted it out last night, but my younger sister, Hope, died in March." The words still stuck in her throat as if saying them somehow made it more real.

He squeezed her hand. "I'm sorry, Bristol."

She looked out the window at the winter woods as it blurred by but didn't slip her hand out of his. "Thanks. It's been tough. And this crazy hockey thing is the first thing that's put a smile on my daughter's face since then. So I need to figure out a way to turn myself into a great coach."

"How are *you* doing?" he asked.

"I'm fine," she said automatically.

"That sounded convincing."

Bristol shrugged. "I'm lost and empty and sad and damn tired of feeling all those things. The missing her just sneaks up on me and hits me in the backs of the knees sometimes, you know? And the rest of the time I'm numb. It's like life lost its color when she died."

"And you're frustrated that you're still hurting," he guessed.

"I hate feeling empty, but I hate feeling helpless even more. I can't make my mom stop sneaking off to cry in the kitchen when we're all over for dinner because there's an empty chair. I can't make Savannah stop hurting because Hope won't be standing up there next to us at her wedding. And I can't stop worrying that, eventually, everyone's going to forget that she ever existed. Everyone except us."

"That's not going to happen." He said it with a certainty that she longed to feel.

"How can you be so sure?" Bristol hated the catch in her voice. But at least hate was better to feel than nothing.

"You said your sister saved lives."

"She was an EMT. She was going to be a doctor."

"Every single person she saved or helped or made a differ-ence to will remember her for the rest of their lives. Same as you."

"Same as me how?"

"Oh how quickly you forget." His eyes crinkled at the corners when he smiled. "Bristol, you saved that coach's life yesterday. Do you think he's going to ever forget that?"

"That was just right time, right place. There's nothing heroic about—"

"There is nothing that you or anyone else in this world can do that's more important than giving life. Whether it's parent-hood or CPR or brain surgery, you have no idea the lives you touch."

There was something in his tone that she tuned into, a raw pain or passion. She wasn't sure which.

"I hope you're right. It would do us all some good to know that she mattered to more than just our family. Our neighbors have been amazing, and I'm so grateful for everything they've done. It's just hard to see the world move on while you're still leveled."

Beau brought her gloved hand to his lips and kissed her knuckles, and despite the pain that bloomed cold and bright inside her whenever she spoke of Hope, she felt a thrill race through her. "I promise you, your sister will be remembered."

Bristol found his words oddly comforting.

"Thanks, Beau."

He lowered their joined hands but didn't let go.

She was holding hands with a man who had stepped up for her in more ways than she could count in the last twenty-four hours. And she felt... something. The numbness had made room for something warm, something bright.

Bristol cleared her throat. "So how about your family?"

She caught the grimace out of the corner of her eye. "My family is... weird. We're not close. My parents haven't really been in my life since I was twenty."

"Divorce?"

He shook his head. "No, nothing like that. They're actually pretty incredible people. They started a foreign aid nonprofit and left the country years ago. They move around from country to country, drawing attention to human aid crises and fundraising for special projects. They're very passionate about what they do, but they weren't as passionate about maintaining a relationship with their kids."

"You have siblings?" Bristol asked.

"A sister. She's a lot younger than me. Eleven years younger, and she came to live with me when my parents left."

"Wow."

"Yeah, talk about an adjustment period for us both. But we made it work."

"That's amazing that you were able to step in and be a parent like that."

He shot her an amused look. "I might point out that that's

incredibly sexist of you. How old were you when you had your daughter?"

Bristol opened her mouth to protest and then closed it again. "Twenty."

"Hmm, what a coincidence."

"I could argue that getting knocked up biologically forces you to mentally prepare for impending motherhood. You, on the other hand, were dumped into it with less preparation."

"I'll grudgingly give you half a point on that. But don't think that makes up for your gross assumption that I'm so much more amazing for becoming a legal guardian for my sister at the same age you became a parent. My sister was potty trained and could make her own lunch."

Bristol laughed, and it felt damn good. "You're an interesting man, Beau French."

His smile faded, and she thought she saw a shadow cross his face. But he didn't let go of her hand.

7

*B*eau swiped the sweat from his forehead with the back of his hand and then unscrewed the cap on his bottle of water. He guzzled several swallows before revisiting his quest to catch his breath.

"That was like walking through hell in bare feet, man," he gasped.

Lucky Dorsey, MMA champion and sadistic trainer, flopped down on the floor next to him. They were only two of the dozen bodies currently littering the floor of the gym across the street from Early Bird.

"Thanks, man," Lucky said, taking a much more leisurely sip of water. "You hung tough. You train?"

Beau shook his head. "Not for a while. I'm hoping to get back into it."

"You're welcome here anytime." Lucky studied Beau over his protein shake. "You look familiar."

Hockey players and MMA athletes didn't usually run in the same circles, but there were always events that overlapped such as the ESPYs and every party *Sports Illustrated* ever threw. It was very possible he and Lucky had crossed paths before, but it wouldn't do him any good if the man made the connection now.

"I have that kind of face... or beard. Unless you frequent yoga studios in Chicago?" he added.

"Not likely," Lucky laughed. "What brings you to town?"

Hope Falls had clearly gotten its hooks in Lucky, Beau thought.

"I'm in town on business," he said evasively.

"Hang on. Beau, right?"

"Yeah," he said with reluctance.

"Beau the guy who saved Coach Tubs. You're staying at my brother's B&B."

"Small town," Beau said weakly.

"No kidding. Watch out or they'll suck you in, too. There's an unusual percentage of people who come for a visit and end up getting their feet knocked out from under them, falling in love, and settling down."

Bristol's smiling face immediately appeared in his mind's eye. Their talk last night had been raw and revealing. And hearing her laugh—really laugh—had hit him hard in the chest. He wanted to listen to that laugh again and again. But he wasn't looking for love, and he sure as hell wasn't looking to uproot his life and move to Hope Freaking Falls.

"I'm sure most escape unscathed."

"That's what I thought, and then I met Deanna running around in the woods shouting my name. She was actually calling a dog," he said with a grin. "I'm a fighter, but even I knew enough to surrender right then and there." He shoved a hand through his sweaty dark hair. "And now I wouldn't have it any other way. Never in a million years would have pictured myself married to a firefighter."

"A firefighter?" Beau asked. "Did she know Hope Quinn?"

"You knew Hope?"

Beau shook his head. "I met her sister, Bristol."

"Right! You and she helped save Tubs. That was good work there."

"Uh, thanks," Beau said, wishing Lucky would get back on topic.

"Yeah, when Hope had time off of school and residencies and whatever she still volunteered as an EMT. Deanna really liked her. But it's hard not to like the Quinns."

"One of those families, huh?"

"Oh, yeah. Big Bob and Mary are great people and that extends to their daughters."

"It must have been a tough year for them," Beau speculated.

"The worst," Lucky shook his head. "I can't imagine going through a loss like that. But the Quinns? They're strong, you know? They're in the ICU when the doctor tells them the news, and they decide right then and there to donate Hope's organs. A time like that for their family, and they're still thinking about others."

Beau felt his throat tighten. "They sound like good people."

"The best. Their oldest daughter is getting married soon. The whole town's invited, and we're all hoping a dose of happy will do them good."

The guilt that had teased at him since he first met Bristol was back and punching him in the gut. He had his reasons for lying. He just hoped Bristol would understand in the end.

"Hey, man. You look like you're gonna puke," Lucky said, looking concerned.

"Must have been the last round on the speed bag," Beau guessed.

"Who's up for breakfast?" A tall guy with wide shoulders dropped a gym bag in front of them. "I'm hitting Early Bird."

"Beau, I'm assuming you've already met Justin here since you're here for the yoga retreat."

Justin cocked his head to one side. "I don't think we've met yet. I'm Justin Barnes. My wife, Amanda, and I run Mountain Ridge," he said, offering a hand.

Shit. Beau hid his wince behind his standard smile-for-the-cameras expression. "Ah, hey. It's nice to meet you."

Justin had a firm shake and a friendly face. "Sorry we haven't met, yet. But there's a lot of you yogis running around out there."

"You have a really nice place here," Beau told him. After Bristol had essentially forced him into the lie about being in town on yoga business, he'd done some online research on Mountain Ridge and its facilities.

"I'm pretty impressed that you're here for this ass-kicking and then heading back for all those workshops."

"Yeah. I'm thinking I might have made a mistake," Beau grimaced. He wasn't talking about exercise anymore.

"Hey, you're a yoga instructor! Why don't you lead us through a stretching sequence for a cool down?" Lucky said, looking like he just had the greatest idea ever.

"That would be awesome," Justin said, rolling his shoulders. "Otherwise I'm gonna be hurting later, and I like my wife thinking that I'm invincible."

Lucky jerked his thumb at Justin. "Another one just passing through that fell into the Hope Falls marriage trap."

"That's not technically true. I grew up here," Justin explained to Beau. "My dad and my little brother live here."

Beau nodded as if enthralled with the conversation. If he could keep them talking, they'd forget all about the impromptu yoga session.

"I was just warning Beau here about the danger to visitors."

Justin nodded seriously. "Dude, watch your back. Marriage is contagious here, so if you're not looking for something serious, keep your head down and get out while you still can."

Lucky snorted. "As if you'd have it any other way."

Justin grinned. "Yeah, it's not so bad. Just keep an eye out. I think there's something in the water here. If you stick around too long, you'll fall hard for someone."

"He already met Bristol," Lucky said helpfully. If the guy wasn't an MMA champion, Beau would have happily punched him in the face.

"Nice." There was a lot of meaning Justin put into that one word. And Beau didn't want to stand around hashing it out.

"I'm just in town for a few days," he told them defensively. "I'm not looking for something permanent." Hell, he had no idea what he was looking for. This past year had been nothing but putting one foot in front of the other. One doctor's appointment after another. Hoping and worrying. He'd left his career behind without a second thought, and with it went the life he'd been comfortably floating through. He'd veered off his predetermined course, a decision he'd never regret.

But now? Now when he'd reached the light at the end of the tunnel, there was one last thing he had to do before he could think about the future. One last promise to keep before moving forward.

"Well let's get this stretching started so I can head over to Early Bird." Justin asked. "Bristol's got a stack of pancakes with my name on it."

"Oh, we don't have to do the yoga thing," Beau began.

"Hey, man. Yoga is an important part of a well-rounded athletic ability." Lucky sounded like he was quoting a trainer. "Listen up, team. Beau here is going to run us through a quick yoga cool down to recover from that beater."

"You don't have to stay if you don't want to," Beau added

hopefully. He swore under his breath when every single one of the men and women stayed put.

He could do this. He'd been team captain. He'd done the requisite yoga training session during preseason. He could fake it, right?

"Uh, okay, let's start by stretching out our calves with... uh, facedown dog..."

~

HOCKEY PRACTICE WASN'T EXACTLY a complete disaster. None of the kids had broken any bones... yet. But that was about all she could put in the positivity column. Two six-year-olds were locked in an epic battle throwing snowballs, gloves, and whatever else they could get their grubby paws on at each other.

One of the seven-year-olds had his finger so far up his nose she thought he might be mining brain. The rest of them, Violet included, were careening around on the ice like a pinball game in sugared up human form.

She was thankful that their practices took place on King's Pond instead of the bustling rink just outside of town. There were fewer people here to witness how truly bad the Polar Bears and their new coach were.

Despite the impending disaster of a hockey season, all Bristol could think about was the fact that Beau hadn't come in for breakfast this morning. Justin Barnes and Lucky Dorsey had and told her they'd met Beau at the gym for the five a.m. class. But he hadn't joined them for breakfast. He hadn't come to see her.

It shouldn't bother her. Should it? *They weren't seeing each other. Heck, they weren't even friends*, she reasoned. They were acquaintances. And she was being an idiot. She was acting like her second grade self when she had that embarrassing crush on Jake Maguire, now Hope Falls' hunky fire chief and husband of her friend and artist-of-the-month Tessa Hayes.

Well, it was no use pouting or ruminating over Beau French. She had work to do. Somehow.

"Guys!" Bristol shouted through gloved fingers. "Gather around."

Violet skated over to her, dragging a giggling girl behind her. "What do you want us to do, Mom?"

She wanted them to magically become a professional hockey team. Or, better yet, say they didn't want to play hockey anymore.

Was that too much to ask?

"How do I make them do stuff?" she asked, pointing at the chaos.

"I don't know," Violet shrugged. "You're a mom. Shouldn't you know this stuff?"

"Crap," Bristol said under her breath.

"Forget your whistle, coach?"

She turned on her skates so fast that she almost fell, saving herself at the last possible second by hooking an arm awkwardly over the boards lining the pond's makeshift rink.

Beau, looking sexier by the second, rested his elbow on the wall.

"Please, for the love of God, tell me you're here to help," she begged.

"It'll cost you," he warned.

"I don't care what it costs! Get over here and tell me what to do!"

"I'm willing to bet every cent in my bank account that that's the first time in your life you've ever uttered those words."

"Beau!"

"Okay, okay." He held up his hands. "Let me put my skates on."

Bristol's sigh of relief was short lived. She needed her next inhale to yell at Mickey Raspon, who was wielding his hockey stick like a baseball bat and chasing his little brother who had inexplicably wandered onto the ice. "Hey! Everyone over here, now!"

The mom voice worked and had her rag tag crew of mini hockey wannabes skating over to surround her in a loose circle.

"Okay, guys, as you know, Coach Tubs had to take some time off," she began.

Noah Barnes raised his hand. "It's 'cause he had a heart attack and almost died," he announced, with the wisdom of a six-year-old.

A collective "whoa" rose from the team.

"Coach Tubs is going to be fine," Bristol said, reassuring them. "But I'll be your coach for the rest of the season. Do you have any questions?"

Hands shot up everywhere.

"What should we call you? Coach Violet's Mom?" a little girl in pink leggings and matching hockey skates asked as she scraped her brown curls back from her face.

"How about Coach Quinn?" Beau skated up and stopped next to her sending a shower of ice slivers toward the kids earning another collective "whoa." Even Bristol was impressed. There was something graceful about the way he moved on and off the rink.

The kids immediately scattered attempting to recreate Beau's entrance, skidding and sliding around the rink.

"Nice, Beau. Now we're going to have to round them up again," Bristol sighed.

He held up a whistle on a cord and dangled it in front of

her face. "All kids are programmed to respond to a whistle. They either stop what they're doing, or they start doing what you told them to."

She stared at him for a beat.

"What? I'm serious. Try it." He wiggled the cord.

Bristol snatched the whistle out of his fingers and blew a sharp, shrill tweet. The kids froze and then began to meander back to her.

"Huh," she said. "It worked."

"You're welcome."

"Quick, what do I do when they get back?"

"Tell them to get ready for a skating drill. Get them in two lines, and I'll take care of the rest."

"Skating drill. Two lines. Got it." Bristol nodded. "Okay, guys, we're going to do a skating drill..."

8

"*B*ye, Coach Quinn! Bye Coach Beau!"

The kids packed up and rolled away in minivans and SUVs with whatever carpooling parents had drawn the short straw that day.

Bristol waved them off while Violet chased Beau in and out of the little orange traffic cones they'd set up on the ice. Practice had been an eye-opening experience. The Polar Bears were bad at skating, passing, shooting, and probably defense too. The only thing they excelled at was gravity and whining.

The odds of her leading them to a victorious season was about the same as discovering that she was the long-lost heir to the throne in a teeny tiny European monarchy.

Bristol felt a sense of pride when she managed to skate over to where Beau and Violet were playing without falling on her face or her ass.

"Good job today, Mom," Violet grinned, pulling up to a stop in front of her.

"Thanks, Vi. You're really getting good at skating!"

"I know! Hey, watch this," her daughter chirped whizzing by to skate circles around Beau.

God, if only she had an ounce of that confidence... and energy... and damn balance on ice, Bristol thought.

Beau gave chase to Violet and the two scrambled over the ice laughing and taunting each other. Bristol picked her way through the cones, tucking them under her arm as she went.

She felt the late afternoon air begin to warm and knew Beau was approaching. "You ready for your lesson?" he asked, gliding up to her, Violet on his heels.

"We're gonna teach you, Mom. Okay?"

Bristol ruffled the purple pom-pom on Violet's hat, one Hope had given her for Christmas the year before. The one Vi had worn until June before finally letting Bristol pack it up until winter returned.

"You already helped me through practice," she told Beau, lamely. "You don't need to stick around."

Beau looked down at Violet and crossed his arms. "I think someone's trying to get out of class."

Violet copied his stance. "Yeah, Mom. Come on! It'll be fun!"

"I feel a little guilty taking up all your free time while you're here," she confessed.

"Bristol, it's Hope Falls. It's not like you're keeping me from an exciting nightlife."

"But I'm sure there are events going on at Mountain Ridge that you're missing out on."

"It's a yoga retreat. They're pretty flexible." He winked.

"Ha."

"Come on, Mom! Stop stalling!"

Bristol looked at her watch. "Fine, but we're calling it a night at six."

"Good. Are you ready, Coach Violet?"

"Ready, Coach Beau!"

They ran her through a few skating drills focusing on stopping, starting, and—when her performance was deemed acceptable—turning. And as she slid and skidded her way around the ice, Beau quizzed her on hockey terminology.

She had no idea what red line icing was, but she understood the concept of a penalty box. "A time out seat," as Violet had helpfully explained it.

She was going to need a crash course before Wednesday's game, but at least her feet were steadier.

"Who in the world ever decided, 'Oh hey, I need to cross this frozen body of water. Let me strap knives to my feet?'" she demanded breathlessly as she finished her final quarter-speed sprint to the rink's gate where Beau and Violet waited patiently. "An idiot, that's who!"

She misjudged her speed and then her stopping ability and plowed into Beau knocking him flat on his back. She landed on top of him with an "oomph" driving the air out of them both. Beneath her, his body was even less forgiving than the ice.

Violet doubled over with laughter, her blonde braids swinging from under her hat.

"Body checking's an advanced lesson, Ace," Beau told her.

"Sorry," Bristol gasped, trying to crawl off of him. But his hands clamped down on her hips holding her in place.

"Don't move," he whispered through clenched teeth.

"Oh, crap. Did I hurt you?" But she suddenly felt the reason for his demand stir to life hard against her thigh.

"Shit," he muttered, dropping his head back on the ice.

Bristol went from cold to flaming hot in the half-second it took to see the desire light his green eyes. Sprawled atop him, she could feel his breath on her face, could see the strain of want and need in the clench of his jaw.

"Mom! I'm hungry," Violet complained in a singsong voice, obviously over the humor of their physical comedy.

"Yeah, uh. Me, too, kid," Bristol said, not taking her eyes off of Beau. His fingers flexed in her hips, and it felt so incredibly good. She wanted to stay here draped over Beau for the rest of forever. But not with her daughter watching and not on a rapidly cooling November night. She wanted to be in a bed, moving over him under sheets—

Get a damn hold of yourself, she snapped internally.

"One of us is going to have to move," she whispered finally.

"I swear I usually have more control than this," he gritted out.

She bit her lip to cover her laugh.

"Don't you dare laugh at this," he warned her. "You'll scar me for life."

"No laughing, no scarring," she agreed, not bothering to keep the humor out of her voice.

"Okay, on three, I'm going to lift you off. Got it?"

She braced her hands against his chest. "Got it."

"One, two, three." He lifted her from the hips as if she weighed nothing.

Bristol was able to regain her feet and distract Violet with the important task of finding her bag and the car keys while Beau got up and thought about whatever men think about in situations like that.

"Well, that was embarrassing," Beau said, running a hand through his thick hair. "Definitely the last time I ever wear sweatpants to practice."

Bristol couldn't stop herself from looking down *there*. "Wow."

She slapped a hand over her mouth. *Had she really just said that out loud?* The flush that rose on her cheeks had zero to do with the wind chill or the ice.

"Hey. Eyes up here, Quinn," Beau ordered.

Bristol spun around to force herself to stop looking at him.

"Hey, Mom! You looked just like an ice skater!" Violet's applause was muffled by her mittens.

"I didn't fall!" Bristol carefully eased back around to face Beau. She shot her arms up in victory. "I'm so awesome!"

His grin, quick and sexy, had that warm gooey feeling sliding through her belly again.

"Hey, Beau! Are you hungry?" Violet called from the gate.

"Is ice cold?"

"Yes! Come have dinner with us!"

Bristol and Beau stared at each other for a long time. She was surprised that the heat sparking off of them didn't melt the ice under their feet.

"Would you like to come to dinner, Beau?" Bristol asked him, keeping her voice low enough that Violet couldn't overhear.

He nodded, his eyes serious. "Yeah, I would."

"Are you coming with us, Beau?" Violet demanded.

"That depends—what's for dinner?"

9

They parted ways in the parking lot, and Bristol zipped home to give herself enough time to change clothes and hide any clutter that lurked about the apartment. She hustled Violet inside and sent her on a mission to hide any piles of anything before dashing off into her bedroom to assault her closet.

Bristol settled on a pair of distressed skinny jeans and a button-down flannel. Casual, but cute. She yanked her hair out of its ponytail and ran her fingers through the roots for a little lift and tousle. She slicked on a layer of lip-gloss and deemed herself good to go just in time for Violet's seventh hunger statement since they left the rink.

"I was going to make tacos. Do you think Beau will like tacos?" she asked Violet, who shrugged helpfully.

"Mom, who doesn't like tacos?"

"Good point. How much homework do you have?"

"Ummmmm..."

Bristol could tell by the way Violet studiously avoided her gaze while waltzing around the apartment that it wasn't a light night.

"Go get your books and start working at the table. I'll start dinner."

"But, Mom!"

"Nice try. Books, kid."

While Violet stomped off toward her room lamenting about the unfair life of an eight-year-old, Bristol launched herself into food prep. She'd make chicken and beef tacos in case Beau was a red meat kind of guy. He sure looked like one. Her brain unfailingly revisited the scene on the ice, and Bristol took a steadying breath. *What was this feeling?* she wondered. And then it hit her. It was *feeling.* She wasn't frigidly, fragilely numb. There was a thaw happening inside her, a melting of the ice that had formed on her heart all those months ago.

As she tossed chicken breast with spices, Bristol's gaze flickered over to the photo of Hope at her college graduation on the wall next to the framed picture of Vi's preschool graduation. Was she being unfaithful to her grief? Was it too soon to be feeling something happy, something interesting?

Bristol turned on the range and shook her head. If her sister could see her now, Hope would probably slap her upside the head. She knew with certainty that Hope would be hurt by their bottomless devastation. But Bristol—and the rest of the family—seemed to have no idea how to move past the hurt to get somewhere, anywhere else.

Was Beau a catalyst? she wondered. *Could having feelings for him open her heart from its hibernation?*

Violet stomped back in lugging her backpack.

"History tonight?" Bristol asked sympathetically.

Violet sighed dramatically. "Yeah. Five whole questions to answer. Like anyone even cares what happened a bajillion years ago." She dropped down into a chair at the dining table and unceremoniously dumped the contents of her backpack.

Bristol diced onions and tomatoes in silence. She knew better than to try to talk Violet out of her funks. It was better to acknowledge the feelings and then let Violet work them out. Unless of course she was being a grumpy punk, in which case Bristol was more than happy to step in.

It was a benefit of being a young-ish mom, she thought. She was close enough to really get that the big things in Violet's life really were the big things. A lost balloon, an unkind friend on the playground, those were the equivalents of lost jobs and breakups in adulthood. And if Violet could trust Bristol to be there for her now, she could keep on trusting her when the upsets got bigger.

When she'd found out she was pregnant at twenty, she'd panicked. She had a plan, and a baby didn't fit into that plan, not then at least. Neither had a hasty marriage. But thanks to the support of her family, Bristol had managed to graduate on time with a degree in business management. Hope had given up her summers at eighteen and nineteen and taken care of her beautiful baby niece while Bristol went to school and Nolan worked odd jobs. Savannah, who'd been working her way through law school, had sent Bristol a small check every week to "help out with necessities." And everywhere else, Bob and Mary Quinn had stepped up.

She'd graduated exhausted but proud and vowed that she would never give a one of them reason to regret their support. She glanced over at Violet hunched over her books, a frown on her pretty face, and wondered if her daughter knew how loved she had been from the very first moment.

Bristol browned the ground beef in one pan while the chicken sizzled in a second. She ran a knife through the fresh cilantro and dragged sour cream, cheeses, and salsa from the fridge.

"What the hell am I going to do for dessert?" she muttered.

"Hot chocolate, duh!" Violet said, looking up from her homework.

"Vi, if I haven't said it enough today, you're a genius," Bristol said, air-fiving her daughter from the kitchen.

Violet reluctantly raised her hand for the five. "You know, Janessa Mingle's mom does her homework for her," she began, blue eyes big and hopeful.

"Janessa Mingle's mom isn't concerned about Janessa growing up to be a self-sufficient adult. She's worried about Janessa being an eight-year-old with straight A's."

A knock at the door cut off their routine argument. Janessa also had her own cell phone, a purple canopy bed, and two hamsters. It was hard not being Janessa.

Bristol brushed her hands over her jeans and hauled ass down the hall. She pulled open the door and felt her heart skip seeing Beau on her doorstep.

He'd changed into jeans and an expensive-looking sweater that might be cashmere. Casual, but upscale. The look suited him.

"I had no idea you lived above the restaurant," Beau said when she ushered him inside. "I thought you had me pick you up here because you were working. This place is amazing."

"Thanks," she said, taking his coat and tucking it into the hall closet. "This is home. I can't beat the commute."

"Do you slide down the bannister when you're running late?"

"All the time." She grinned up at him and just enjoyed the feel of having him in her space.

"I brought this for you," he said, holding out a bottle of wine.

"You didn't have to do that," she began.

He reached over and squished her cheeks with one hand.

"That's very nice of you, Beau. Thank you," he said in a falsetto tone, making her mouth work like a guppy.

Bristol rolled her eyes. "Thank you, Beau," she repeated.

"You're welcome," he said, his fingers lingering on her jaw.

"Hi, Beau!" Violet rocketed down the hallway to greet him.

"Hey, Vi," Beau greeted her with enthusiasm so sincere Bristol felt her heart do a little flip-flop. *Get a hold of yourself, Quinn. He's here for tacos, not a lifetime together.*

"Hey, Violet, would you mind giving Beau the grand tour while I finish dinner?"

"Sure! Come on, Beau. I'll show you my room!" Violet grabbed his arm and started dragging him down the hallway toward her door.

Bristol winked at him as she headed back to the kitchen. She always enjoyed watching people experience her place for the first time. It was such an eclectic space with the sky-high ceilings and the scarred floors, the timeworn brick and the exposed ducting. It didn't suit everyone's tastes. There was no formal dining room, no wall-to-wall carpeting. But the sheer amount of space, the hours of natural light that the arched windows let in, made up for the lack of conventionality.

Bristol couldn't imagine living anywhere else. And maybe someday it would feel like home again.

"This is my closet. There's a bunch of clothes in there. And this is where I keep most of my games," Violet said, pointing at a bookcase. "Have you ever played Mud Battle?"

Beau didn't have a chance to answer before she was scrambling up onto the shelf like a ladder to reach for one of the game boxes.

"Whoa there, short stack," he said making a grab for her when the bookcase swayed. Violet giggled when he plucked her off the shelf with one arm and steadied the bookcase with the other. "Let's go see if your mom has a drill and some screws."

They started down the hallway, and Violet pointed at the closed door on the left. "That's my mom's room. It's really nice. It has a h-u-u-u-ge bath tub."

Beau didn't need that information. Not after their "moment" on the ice. Anything involving a naked Bristol should be strictly off limits. "How about this room?" he asked, pointing at the next door.

Violet's face fell. "Oh, that's my Aunt Hope's room. She's not alive anymore."

"I'm sorry. She lived with you?"

"You're sorry she lived with us?" Violet frowned in confusion.

"No," Beau smiled. "I'm sorry your aunt isn't here anymore." Her slim shoulders were slumped, and Beau felt like the ultimate ass.

"Yeah, me too," she sighed.

"She was pretty great, huh?"

"She was kind of the best. She had curly hair, and she made really good popcorn."

"That sounds like the best," he agreed.

They entered the large space at the end of the hall that smelled like spices and meats and baking taco shells. "Mom, Beau wants a screw."

The spatula in Bristol's hand fell to the floor.

"A drill and screws," he corrected. "For the bookcase in short stack's room."

Bristol blinked. "*Those* screws. Right. Um, here." She handed him a fresh spatula. "Make sure this doesn't burn, and

I'll be back." She dashed out of the kitchen, and Violet dragged a schoolbook over to the island.

Beau grabbed the dishtowel off the counter, threw it over his shoulder and stirred the chicken with finesse.

"Homework?" he asked.

"History," she sighed with all the regret that a person of her worldly experience could muster.

"Not your favorite subject?"

"I like science and gym and lunch and art."

Beau turned down the flames on the burners and pulled the taco shells out of the oven. "History was my favorite class. Besides gym."

"Are you serious?" Violet looked as though she was trying to decide if he was lying to her. "Who cares about old people who did old stuff?"

"Short stack, history is all the stuff that came before us. Think about it, if it weren't for history, none of us would be here. This building wouldn't even be here. Where does your mom keep the thing that opens the wine?"

Violet pointed to a drawer. "So, old stuff is important?"

"You tell me," he said, turning the corkscrew. "You live in this cool building. It's old. Some people don't have all these big windows and these high ceilings. Some people can't ride their scooters around their living rooms."

She still looked skeptical. "See, when you care about history, you care about the people who made it. The person who built this building. The general who led troops into battle. The first people who climbed a mountain. Whoever invented hockey."

"Someone invented hockey?" The realization dawned bright in those blue eyes.

"Someone invented everything or discovered it," he said, opening cabinets until he found the wine glasses. He pulled two down and filled them. Then he took a third one and filled it with water before sliding it across the counter to Violet.

"Wow, you really like history," Violet said, picking up her glass with delight.

"I really like people."

"Found it!" Bristol returned lugging a green plastic tote. She hefted it onto the counter and yanked off the lid. Beau hazarded a look inside and raised an eyebrow. Inside was a tangle of handheld tools and miscellaneous tool-related accessories.

"What?" Bristol asked, daring him to criticize. "This is Pops' tool tote. We put him to work when he visits, don't we Vi?"

"We used to use Mr. Maybry next door at the hardware store," Violet put in. "But then they closed it. I miss Mr. Maybry. He used to bring me lollipops."

"That was a hardware store next door?" Beau asked, handing Bristol a glass of wine.

"The Pollard family owned it for something like seventy years, but when the last owner passed away this summer, none of the kids or grandkids were interested in running it, and they couldn't come to an agreement about selling it. So it sits empty, and poor Mr. Maybry is still out of work," Bristol explained, peeking over Violet's shoulder to check her daughter's work.

"Well, it looks like everything here is done," Beau said, turning off the burners. "Time to eat?"

~

THEY ATE tacos and talked hockey. And Bristol plotted her move.

She'd made up her mind when she'd walked into her

kitchen and seen Beau making himself at home, finishing dinner, and chatting with Violet about the importance of history.

He fit. He fit in her home, in her life, and she was going to seduce him. Bristol felt almost silly planning a fling. By definition, a fling was temporary. Compatibility wasn't a necessity. Hell, it wasn't even a requirement. But Bristol didn't see the point in letting someone into her bed if she wouldn't enjoy them in her life.

And Beau fit. His temporary status in Hope Falls took him off the table for a long-term relationship, so a fling it would be. She hoped it would be a bit flingier than the only other short-term affair she'd attempted. That had been the captain of her college's swim team, and they'd ended up dating seriously, getting pregnant her junior year, and then married.

As far as flings went, Nolan had been a failure. But Beau? He was perfect fling material. She eyed him over her wineglass and when his gaze met hers, she felt a spark of excitement zing up her spine.

Perfect fling material.

He ate six tacos as much out of genuine enjoyment as to entertain Violet. And when they were finished eating, he gave Bristol a crash course in the positions of a hockey team using salt and pepper shakers and a plethora of dinner table items.

"See, you want your fastest right-handed player up on right wing because they'll have the best chance at scoring," he explained.

"Okay, that actually makes sense," Bristol admitted.

"You'll figure this out," he promised. And she would. She

was smart and determined, an unbeatable combination in an opponent and a sexy one in an attraction.

"Vi, let's finish up this homework now so you can relax before bed," Bristol suggested.

Violet grumbled but took her plate into the kitchen where she loaded it into the dishwasher.

"I'll take care of the shelves," Beau volunteered, following Violet's lead and clearing the remaining dishes. He loaded up the dishwasher and headed back the hallway to Violet's room.

It really seemed like a haven for a well-rounded eight-year-old. The walls that were drywall were painted a pale lavender, and there was a thick multi-colored rug that covered most of the floor. There were Legos scattered on the floor and a desk stacked with books, some kind of terrarium, and a microscope. Stuffed animals were spilling out of bins and buckets intended to organize chaos. The white dresser looked like it was exploding with kid clothes.

Beau made quick work of securing the shelves to the wall, and once he was satisfied that the bookcase wouldn't topple over and crush Violet, he took a moment to reorganize the tool tote. Pops would thank him later.

A framed picture on Violet's nightstand caught his eye. Bristol and Violet each had an arm looped around the neck of another woman, their cheeks pressing tight against hers. She was young with springy brown curls and Bristol's high cheekbones and the same exotic tilt to her eyes. She grinned at the camera as if in mid-laugh. He could feel the vitality.

Hope. The picture they'd run with her obituary no more captured the essence of the woman—taken too soon when her car hit a patch of ice—than the text did. But in this picture, Beau could sense the life of the woman who had given him a gift so precious. He'd never be able to thank her, but there were others that he could thank.

"That's my sister Hope," Bristol said. She straightened away from the doorway and joined him.

He handed her the picture. "Pretty like her sister," he commented. There was no dimple when Bristol's lips curved in a sad smile.

"She was the good one," she said, returning the picture to its home angled toward Violet's bed. "Vanna's the smart one, I'm the steady one, and Hope was the good one."

"And you feel like all that's changed because she's gone?"

She looked at him then with those sad eyes, and he felt the connection roll through him fast and deep.

"Yeah, I do," she nodded. "Our whole lives, we were one-third of a trio. That was my identity. I don't know who I am without those anchors."

Beau watched her pull it back and tuck it away with the rest of the pain.

"Sorry. You came for tacos, not sob stories."

"Don't." He said it softly and tucked a soft, silky tress of hair behind her ear. "Don't feel like you're not allowed to be sad." He knew what it was like to keep things locked up tight, to be intensely private even when surrounded by others. Battles fought privately could take more pieces of the soul than one with an army at your back.

"Thanks, Beau," Bristol whispered.

He indulged himself and rubbed a thumb over her full bottom lip. He loved how his name sounded from her mouth.

"Mo-o-om. I'm do-o-one."

Violet's dramatic announcement from the kitchen broke the spell. This time when Bristol smiled at him, Beau was treated to both dimples.

"How do you feel about hot chocolate?" she asked.

"Confused and regretful?"

Bristol laughed and led the way back to the kitchen. "Vi, do you want to help me with the hot chocolate?"

"Can I do the whipped cream?" Violet's blonde head peeked around the corner.

"I hope you like whipped cream," Bristol whispered over her shoulder to Beau.

He did, and he was doing his best not to think about all the ways he'd like to enjoy whipped cream with Bristol.

"Go make yourself comfortable in the living room," Bristol directed. "We'll bring the hot chocolate in there."

He shouldn't be doing this, Beau reminded himself as he stepped into the large space off the kitchen. He wasn't here to get involved or disrupt a family. He was here to observe.

But the minute he'd laid eyes on Bristol Quinn in person, he knew he was in trouble. It had been so easy to find an in with her. Finding her flat on her back on the ice, in need of exactly what he could offer? It was almost as if fate had intervened. But he didn't believe in fate. No, Beau put his faith in hard work and obsessive preparation. But here in Hope Falls, he felt a gentle guiding force shoving him forward when he wanted to pull back.

The tall, arched windows let in the soft glow of Main Street's lampposts. Bristol had kept the large space cozy with comfortable, overstuffed furniture. Pictures and knickknacks, framed art—presumably by Violet—decorated the exposed brick and built-in shelves.

She'd already started decorating for Christmas. Glass trees and red berries covered the mantel of the fireplace, and a large wreath wrapped in twinkle lights and finished with a gold bow hung on the brick wall behind the quilt-draped sofa.

The bones of the loft were surprisingly similar to Beau's own condo in Chicago, soaring ceilings, scarred floors, and the rough texture of original brick. But Bristol had made her space more homey. Home and family were her priorities. She was a caretaker, a woman to believe in and depend on.

He watched Bristol as she trayed up steaming mugs and nudged a dancing Violet toward the living room. They were both laughing, twin dimples on display, and when Bristol's eyes met his, he felt it again, that sharp yearning for *more*.

They were bound together by something stronger than mere physical attraction, something she didn't even know about yet. And he couldn't help but start to reconsider his stance on fate.

They settled on the deep, comfy sofa and drank home-made hot chocolate while the streetlights of Hope Falls twinkled outside the windows.

"Are you coming to our next game, Beau?" Violet asked, a dab of whipped cream decorating her nose.

"Sweetie, that's the day before Thanksgiving. I don't know if Beau will still be in town."

"Actually, I was thinking about sticking around for a little while. I can't miss your first game coaching."

"Really?" Bristol and Violet asked at the same time, their hopefulness mirroring each other.

There was no way he was disappointing those faces.

IT HAD BEEN A PERFECT NIGHT, Beau thought. Not only had he gotten to know Bristol better, but he'd also got to see what her life with Violet was like. And he'd gotten an idea of who Hope had been. Her presence was still felt in Bristol's home.

Bristol walked with him down the long flight of stairs, neither in a hurry to reach their destination.

He turned around, determined to be a polite guest and thank Bristol for a very nice evening. But when he found her stopped on the last step bringing them face-to-face, the words died on his lips.

She looked determined as she wrapped her arms around his neck. Beau felt the soft flannel of her shirt against his skin.

"Thank you for dinner." The words came out mechanically as his brain rushed to catch up with his reality. She was giving him the go-head, loud and clear.

But Beau's first reaction to being handed exactly what he wanted was to second-guess and strategize. On the ice, it was a different story. When the puck came his way, he was always ready, always looking for the back of the net backed by thousands of hours of practice and training.

But in this case, he hadn't laid enough groundwork or made the right preparations, yet.

So it was Bristol who made the move, Bristol who slowly pressed those full, curving lips to his. And it was Bristol who tightened her hold, pulling him closer until their bodies sparked against each other. He tasted chocolate and sweetness and felt the heat of the kiss spread through his body, branding him.

He'd expected the sizzle—had felt it every time they'd touched—but the slow burn that built to an inferno caught him by surprise.

Then it was Beau who was pressing her against the curved wood of the banister and changing the angle of the kiss. It was Beau shifting into the aggressor as he teased her mouth open with his tongue. And when their mouths fused, when their tongues danced, he finally understood what fate was.

10

_B_y the time Wednesday's sun rose on the cold, clear morning, Bristol was pulling Hope's pecan pie out of the oven and swapping it out for the stuffing she'd prepped.

She was on-call downstairs if things got busy, but she was sure Edwin and Maya could handle themselves. Thanksgiving Eve wasn't a big day for Early Bird, but Black Friday was a different story. In the past, she'd dragged Hope out of bed to help with the rush, but that tradition was no longer possible.

Bristol studied the pie and felt the inevitable wave of sadness roll over her.

Thanksgiving, Savannah and Vince's wedding, the first of many happy occasions that they would spend missing Hope. She'd yet to hear back from the recipient of Hope's heart and at this point didn't expect to. It had been a crazy whim, wanting Hope's heart to be there when Savannah walked down the aisle.

Bristol bit her lip and stared at the pie. She picked up her phone, dialed.

"Hi, honey." Her mom's voice sounded tired and sad. Not at

all usual for Mary Quinn, the original early riser. But a mother preparing for a family feast minus one was entitled.

"Hi, Mom," Bristol responded in the same heavy tone. "I made Hope's pie."

"Oh, honey."

That was the thing about her mom. As a romantic, temperamental Italian, the woman *got* things with very little context.

"I haven't cried in a while, but looking at this pie makes me want to cry while I throw it against a wall."

"I've already poured a glass of wine this morning," Mary confessed.

"Mother!" Bristol said in mock horror.

"What? I put it in a coffee mug."

It wasn't a bad idea. Bristol dug out the remains of the bottle of wine that Beau had brought two nights ago. There was a stingy glass left. She poured it into the World's Best Almost Doctor mug she'd gotten Hope.

"No judgment here, Mom. In fact, I'm joining you."

"There's my girl."

"Now, I need you to impart some motherly wisdom on me," Bristol announced. "When is this going to get easier?"

"Hell if I know," her librarian mother sighed. "When you're a parent, you know that bad things can happen. That's why all mothers are insane. We live with the constant fear that something might happen to our kids. But nothing, no amount of fear or precautions, can prepare you for the reality of losing a child."

Bristol wiped away a silent tear with a dishtowel.

"I witnessed every moment of Hope's life. Every smile, every tear, every award, every sarcastic comment about my cooking. And now she's gone."

Bristol heard her mom blow her nose noisily.

"How do you get it to stop hurting?" Bristol sniffled, then sipped.

"You put a Band-Aid on it, and you think about those lives that Hope saved. That's what I do. I think about every person who gets another Thanksgiving with their families because of her, and I'm so grateful that Hope gave them that."

Bristol heaved another sigh, took another sip of wine. "What can I do to help?" she asked.

"Bring your pie, your stuffing, and your game face. I want your father and Vanna to have a good day."

"How much booze are you planning to serve?"

"As much as it takes."

BEAU HAD himself an honest to goodness case of game day nerves. Though it had nothing to do with the game and everything to do with the "after." He'd done nothing for the last two days but think about that kiss. She'd been clear about what she was offering and crystal clear last night.

Violet had tagged along with Bristol to their evening lesson, so there hadn't been an opportunity for a repeat good-bye kiss. But after Violet was tucked into the backseat and the door closed soundly, Bristol had invited him to her apartment. Tonight. She hadn't even said for dinner. In a longstanding Quinn tradition, Violet would be spending the night at her grandparents' after the game. And he would be welcome to spend the night at Bristol's.

His nerves were reaching Stanley Cup proportions.

There was just one small snag. Bristol thought he was Beau French, yoga instructor, not Beau Evanko, retired hockey player.

There was no way he could take her to bed under that

pretense. He'd never lied to get a woman into bed, and he certainly wasn't going to start now, not with her.

He pushed through the glass door of the rink, and everything immediately evened out. The cold, the smell of the ice—no matter where he was, walking into a rink was like coming home.

He spotted Justin Barnes, Noah's older brother, in the crowd and waved. Behind the Polar Bears' bench, he spotted an older couple that he recognized as Bristol's parents. He wondered guiltily if they knew what their daughter's plans were for the evening. He couldn't remember the last time he'd met a girl's parents.

Bristol was there, fortifying the early arrivals with juice boxes and crackers. She was dressed in jeans, a thermal shirt, and thick navy blue vest. Her waterfall of rich brown hair spilled out of a cute wool hat. He felt that punch in his gut when she laughed at something one of the kids said to her. The want that he felt in that moment went deeper than just sex. He'd be happy to see that smile on that face for the rest of his life.

When she spotted him, her face lit up like he was her personal hero riding to her rescue, and Beau knew then and there that he'd do anything he could to make her look at him that way forever.

It was going to have to be one hell of an explanation.

Beau pushed it aside as the kids called out greetings. Their enthusiasm gave him hope that maybe a good game would pave the way to an accepted apology.

"Hey, guys," he said in greeting.

"Coach Beau!" A boy with a Sponge Bob Band-Aid on his jaw skated up. "Louisa forgot her shoulder pads, an' her dad went home to get them."

"Cool," Beau said. With his job as chief information officer fulfilled, Sponge Bob skated off.

"Louisa's our goalie, and Tucker plays something close to our goal," Bristol said, sliding up next to him. "And I am so glad to see you."

"I thought you were just happy not to be in skates."

"Cute."

"I'm glad you think so," he said stroking a hand through his beard and preening.

Bristol shook her head and stared out on the ice where the team warm-up consisted of seeing who could slide the farthest on their knees. She was nervous, and he found that adorable.

"You're going to do fine," he assured her.

"I just really don't want to screw this up for Violet."

"You're not going to screw this up. I won't let you," he promised.

"Thanks, Beau." She was looking at him with so much hope, so much gratitude, that he felt the guilt lodge back into place like an iceberg easing into the pit of his stomach. She arched an eyebrow then. "You're still coming over tonight, right?"

He cleared his throat trying to dislodge the guilt that had settled there. "If you still want me to."

"Oh, I still want you," she grinned.

Their gazes held for a long moment before he forced himself to look away. "Come on. Let's go coach a hockey team."

They ran the Polar Bears through a warm-up on the ice, and Beau hid his smile at Bristol's pep talk, an attempt to manage the team's expectations.

"We're here to have a good time. Remember that. We want to go out there, have fun, and do our best. You never have to be sorry for doing your best."

The kids looked back at her expectantly.

"What do they want?" she whispered to Beau.

"They want to know the lineup."

"Oh, crap. I didn't do a lineup!" she hissed.

"Relax." Beau handed her a clipboard. "It's all here. All three periods, plus substitutions."

She stared down at the papers and then back up at him. "You are my hero. You're my knight on shining ice skates."

God, he hoped she could hold onto that feeling later tonight.

Beau leaned over her. "This is the position, and the kid at the top of the list is the starter."

Bristol laughed. "Braces, Freckles, Short One, Never Shuts Up, and Violet?"

"I didn't catch all their names at practice the other day," he admitted sheepishly.

"That's okay, I think I can figure these out." Bristol said with a wink. "I'm so going to make this worth your while tonight."

The promise electrified the air between them, and as Beau's cock went raging hard, he was pleased with the length of the coat that he chose that day.

"Gorgeous, you've got to stop looking at me like that or else we're going to end up emotionally scarring several generations of Hope Falls residents," he breathed.

She blushed, and when she peeked up at him again, Beau caught the flash of dimple.

"Okay, Polar Bears, listen up..."

~

THE LONGBOTTOM FROZEN ZOMBIES—THEY'D let the kids choose the name— was a brand new team and closely matched the Polar Bears in ability... or lack thereof.

Bristol shuffled through her papers. "Okay, Lenny, you're going to sub in for Valerie at—" she consulted the paper again. "Right defenseman. Do you know what to do?"

Lenny shrugged his shoulders and wrinkled his freckled nose. "Keep the Zombies from scoring?" he guessed.

Bristol flipped back to the handy position dictionary Beau had written for her. "Pretty much, yep."

"'K."

She looked back at the action on the ice. The first period went mercifully scoreless, though not for lack of trying on the Zombies' part. They had dominated the ice but thankfully had terrible aim when it came to shots on goal.

Louisa had deflected the handful of shots that had actually angled toward the net and made Bristol feel like the girl wasn't in the entirely wrong position like the rest of the team. The best thing she could say about the Polar Bears was they weren't falling down as much this period.

Beau watched the action at her side.

Suddenly the Zombies made a breakaway down the ice. The little boy with the puck couldn't have been more than six years old, and Bristol winced when, for no apparent reason, his feet got tangled up, and he face-planted on the ice. The girl behind him skirted around his prone body like a roller derby queen and picked up the puck.

Violet and another Bear gave chase, but the Zombie, with her pigtails and fierce freckled face, zoomed toward the net.

Bristol covered her eyes and peeked through her gloves. The girl took a swing at the puck and missed, but as the crowd released a sigh of relief, she recovered and dinked it into the back of the net.

"Crap," Bristol muttered. She set the good sportsman example by applauding politely for the other team as the players returned to center ice. "Good job, guys," she said lamely.

The Zombies put two more in the net before the end of the second period, and it was a dejected pack of Polar Bears that skated off the ice.

Violet stepped into the box and slumped down on the bench. Not even Pops' funny faces against the glass could cheer her up.

"What do I do?" Bristol asked Beau in desperation.

He grabbed the clipboard out of her hand and ripped up the lineup. "Got a pen?"

She fished one out of her purse and handed it over, watching him scribble away.

"Okay, Polar Bears!"

Beau's rousing shout had Bristol jumping out of her skin.

"We're getting beat now, but that's okay because we were hibernating, and now we're awake and we're hungry!" he announced with the enthusiasm of a Japanese game show host.

The kids stared at him blankly.

"Who's hungry?" Beau yelled.

"Uh, me. I am," Bristol announced, raising her hand slowly. "I am hungry."

"Coach Quinn and I are hungry!" Beau roared. "Who else is hungry?"

"I'm hungry!" Violet raised her hand enthusiastically.

Bristol was fairly certain Violet was being literal, but it was nice to see her getting into the spirit.

"Me, too," Noah piped up. "Got any more crackers?"

"We don't need crackers," Beau shouted. "We eat Zombies!"

That got the rest of the team going. In seconds, he had the entire team on their feet chanting, "We're hungry!"

He was a natural leader and, with his contagious enthusiasm, had the Bears fans on their feet joining the chant. She was staring at a gorgeous Apollo of a man working a bunch of kids into a competitive frenzy, and she couldn't stop smiling. She glanced over her shoulder at her parents and Savannah wildly cheering. Savannah nodded in Beau's direction, and Bristol nodded back. A sly, approving smile spread across her sister's face.

"Okay! We're gonna go out there, and we're going to eat some Zombies! And then after the game, we're going for ice cream or the reasonable equivalent if Hope Falls doesn't have an ice cream place," Beau announced. "Who's with me?"

"Me!" the team screeched in pandemonium.

"Good! Now Coach Quinn and I are making some changes to the lineup. Huddle up!" They huddled around Beau as he handed out new assignments before they took the ice with newfound enthusiasm.

Bristol watched Violet skate to right wing and felt a fresh flutter of parental nerves rise up in her belly.

"Beau are you sure she should be up there?"

"Are you asking as an overprotective mother or a coach who doesn't want to be showing favoritism?"

"Oh, God. Both?"

He slung an arm around her shoulders and squeezed. "Trust me, okay?"

"Well, you've never let me down before in the history of our acquaintance," she joked.

She saw the shadow that passed over his face, but the referee was blowing her whistle, and the action started again.

The hungry Bears had obviously come to play this period. Tucker snatched the puck away from the Zombies' offense and, with an unintentional but enthusiastic ricochet, fed it up toward Violet. Vi skated along the boards at full bore after the puck, and the crowd cheered when she got her stick on it.

But the cheers were short-lived. A Zombie ran into Violet at half speed, and together they went down in a tangle of sticks and limbs.

The fans "oohed" their disappointment... or sympathy. Bristol wasn't sure which was which.

Violet regained her feet and threw a cheery wave in Bristol's direction, which she returned weakly. Five minutes into the period, the Polar Bear fans were on their feet again. Noah had chugged his way up the ice unchallenged and was lining up a shot on goal. A Zombie defensive player appeared out of nowhere and scrambled for the puck.

In the clumsy exchange, the puck escaped through the player's legs and slowly slid toward Violet.

"Take the shot, short stack!" Beau's voice carried across the ice, and Bristol saw the determined set of Violet's shoulders.

"Oh, crap. Oh, crap," Bristol whispered.

Violet drew her stick up and back and let it fly. The puck sailed into the back of the net, and Bristol screamed along with the rest of the crowd. Violet turned around and stared at the bench in shock before she was mauled by all the Bears on the ice. The crowd was on its feet, and Bristol, in the heat of the moment, threw her arms around Beau's neck.

He picked her up and spun her around while the crowd continued to cheer. Bristol waved to her parents who were on their feet jumping for joy.

"Vi-o-let! Vi-o-let!"

Bristol's eyes welled up. "They're cheering her name." She just wanted them all to bask in the moment of pure joy, their first in so long. "My baby scored the first goal of the season, and they're cheering her name."

LUCY SCORE

"Way to go, Coach," Beau said against her ear, his beard tickling her neck.

"This was all you," she grinned. "I'm buying you ice cream."

"With hot fudge?" he asked, lowering her to her feet.

Bristol gave him a wink. "But not too hot. I don't want it to burn my skin." She enjoyed watching the realization wash over him and then a primal heat light up those green eyes.

"Remind me not to operate heavy machinery around you," he said, quietly. "The persistent loss of blood flow to my brain is probably dangerous."

"Do we really have to be there for ice cream? Can't we just give Louisa the credit card and say 'have at it'?" Bristol wondered.

Beau's smile held all the dark promises of a night she wouldn't soon forget, and she felt her own blood jump to simmering.

"I think there would be talk if we didn't show up. The town might send out a search party and imagine what they'd walk in on," he teased.

Bristol laughed, flushing at the thought. Tonight, she was taking Beau to bed, and she just might find a few missing pieces to herself in the whole enjoyable process. The anticipation was waking something inside her, something she thought had disappeared long ago.

11

The rest of the game pushed all thoughts of a private celebration to the back of Bristol's mind. Beau's new lineup seemed to unlock the hidden potential of every player. And by the final buzzer, Violet had scored a second goal, and on her final sprint up the ice, passed the puck to Noah for his first goal.

It was pandemonium in the Bears section.

"Listen," Beau said, suddenly serious as parents—whose only hockey season excitement to date had been the time Tucker had fallen down and gotten so tangled in the goal's net that someone had to break out the scissors—celebrated the thrill of victory. "I need to talk to you about something before... before."

If he told her he was married, she was going to kill him with an ice skate.

"Mo-o-om!" Violet jumped into Bristol's arms, nearly toppling her over. "Did you see?"

Bristol lost track of Beau as the team and parents met in a celebratory lump, clogging the aisles and stairs. While she chatted with all of the cowardly parents who had turned down the coaching spot, she heard someone calling Beau's name. She watched Beau approach a boy from the other team and his parents.

The boy looked like he was staring at Santa on Christmas Eve as he reverently held up a piece of paper to Beau. She saw Beau sneak a glance around before angling his back to the crowd and taking the paper.

She was curious how he'd run into someone he knew when he was a virtual stranger in town, but her curiosity was shoved aside when her parents fought through the crowd to get to her.

Violet threw her arms around her Pops, and they began an animated discussion of just how awesome Violet and hockey were.

Mary slid her arm through Bristol's and smiled. She wore ear warmers in a vibrant shade of purple with a matching scarf wound around her neck. "I wonder if they're going to refreeze the ice after all the heat you and that Beau were throwing off."

"Mother!" Bristol hissed, glancing around them.

"Honey, there's no one in this arena who didn't see those sparks."

"Are we talking about Bristol and Beau?" Savannah jumped in, a soft pretzel in one hand and a coffee in the other."

"Did you even see Violet's goals?" Bristol glared at her sister's smirking face.

"Just because I watched two goals does not mean I missed out on the fireworks off the ice. I saw the way he picked you up like he was going to carry you off to bed. It was hot. How long's he in town?"

The implication was clear. Was Beau in town long enough for a roll in Bristol's hay?

"He's in town for a few more days, I think," Bristol said, hoping the concrete under her feet would open up and she could escape this conversation.

"What's he doing for Thanksgiving? He's not spending it by himself, is he?" Mary demanded.

"I'm not sure—" Bristol began.

"Let's ask him," Savannah decided. She shoved her pretzel into Violet's hands and cupped her free hand around her mouth to yell his name. When he looked up from his conversation with Justin Barnes, she motioned him over.

He made his way through the crowd to Bristol's side, eyes wary.

"Beau, I'm Bristol's sister Savannah, and this is our mom, Mary," Savannah announced. "We want to know what you're doing for Thanksgiving tomorrow."

Beau eyed Bristol before answering. "I haven't given it much thought."

"What about your sister?" Bristol asked.

"She's spending Thanksgiving with our parents in Haiti." The tightness around his mouth told her he wasn't exactly thrilled about that. "But Levi and Shelby are doing up lunch at the B&B for their families. They invited me to join them if I wanted," he continued.

"Don't be silly," Mary said, with a shake of her head. "You'll have lunch with us."

"Oh, I couldn't impose—"

"I'm Italian. It's my life-long wish to feed people," Mary insisted. "You wouldn't deny me my life-long wish, would you?"

Again, Beau's green eyes slid to Bristol, silently begging for help.

"Vi and I would love it if you could come," she admitted.

"And Dad will be thrilled with more testosterone," Savannah interjected.

"Lunch is at one," Mary said. "Plan to be there by noon."

Beau stuffed his hands in his pockets. "Uh, how can I say no?" Bristol hid her smile, knowing the question wasn't entirely rhetorical.

"Beau! Did you see?" Violet jumped out of her grandfather's arms to dance around Beau.

"Two goals and an assist." Beau offered up a high five. "To be honest, I'm not sure which I'm more proud of."

Violet looked at her feet, her ears pink with pleasure. "I figured I already had two goals so why not let Noah take a shot?"

Bristol felt her heart swell with pride. Her kid was kind and fair and loyal. She had to be doing something right as a parent.

"You should be really proud of yourself, short stack. That's team leadership there," Beau told her, and Violet beamed up at him.

"Vi, Beau's coming to Thanksgiving tomorrow," Bristol told her daughter.

"Awesome! Hey, Dad!" Violet waved into the crowd.

Nolan Graber, decked out in a Polar Bears hoodie, grabbed up Violet in a bear hug. "Way to go, Vi-girl! You were awesome!"

Violet giggled as she struggled against his hold. "You're crushing me, Dad!"

"Get used to it, kid. Heroes get crushed in celebration," Nolan said, setting her down on her feet. "So guess what? Lissa got your goals on video."

"No way!"

"Way!" Lissa beamed, balancing a sleeping Lyric on one hip.

Everyone was talking at once, but Bristol found herself focused on Beau. She knew her family situation could be hard to grasp from the outside. But she, Nolan, and Lissa had made parenting Violet their priority, and together they parented as a team.

"Beau, I'd like you to meet Nolan, Violet's dad, and his wife, Lissa. Guys, this is Beau. He keeps rescuing me on the ice."

Nolan offered an enthusiastic handshake. "Great to meet you, Beau. I've heard a lot about you around town."

"Yeah, no one's a stranger for long in Hope Falls," Beau quipped.

"Ain't that the truth," Nolan joked.

Lissa offered her hand. "It's nice to meet a friend of Bristol's."

"Dad, Beau's coming to Thanksgiving tomorrow," Violet announced.

"Awesome!" Nolan high-fived Bob. "More man power, right Pops Quinn?"

Bob Quinn leaned in conspiratorially. "I don't suppose you know six or seven other male yoga instructors you'd like to bring along?" Bob asked hopefully.

"Sorry, sir. Just me," Beau laughed.

"Well, we'll make do," Bob said unconvincingly.

"Dad, it's not that bad," Bristol insisted. "Don't scare Beau away."

"Just how many women will be there?" Beau asked. But no one answered.

Lissa and Savannah each latched onto one of Bristol's arms.

"If you'll excuse us, we need to borrow Bristol for a second," Savannah announced with her may-it-please-the-court smile.

They dragged her a few steps away.

"Girl, tell me you plan to see that man naked," Lissa demanded, shooting an approving look over her shoulder.

Bristol covered the still-sleeping Lyric's ears with her hands.

"Lissa," she hissed.

"Don't play all 'I don't kiss and tell' with us," Savannah warned her. "We've been one step away from signing you up for online dating for months now. If you tell me you don't want to take his pants off, I'm driving you to the hospital and getting a neurologist to examine your head."

Bristol threw another look over her shoulder at Beau who was engaged in conversation with her parents.

"Look, he's coming over to my place tonight, so the sooner we wrap up this victory party and ice cream parade, the sooner I can rip off all his clothes and tell him all of the incredibly dirty things I want him to do to me!"

They stared at her with huge eyes and sky-high eyebrows. One of them started to make the high-pitched squeal that only adult women can muster, and then they were both hugging her.

"I have never loved you more than I do right now," Lissa sighed happily.

"Thank God you're not brain dead—" Savannah cut her own joke off mid-sentence.

"Huh," Bristol said. "Our first brain dead joke since..."

Lissa looked hard at them both and nodded. "I think it went well."

"I agree," Bristol concurred.

"All right then. Let's get you laid," Savannah announced.

"Let's get this show on the road," Lissa yelled, and she and Savannah began to herd the crowd toward the exit.

～

BEAU HAD NEVER SEEN kids eat ice cream so fast. Fifty percent of the team was complaining of brain freeze, but Lissa and Savannah showed no mercy.

"Come on, guys! This is a competition! Who's going to win?" Lissa cheered, bouncing the wide-eyed Lyric on her hip.

Coming off of a tie, apparently the team's first non-loss of the season, the Polar Bears were charged for victory and ate with complete disregard to the side effects. He wondered how many would be puking in the car on the way home.

"Shovel it in, Dad," Savannah prodded Bob. "You're competing, too."

Bristol, for her part, kept her mouth shut and flushed scarlet every time Lissa or Savannah rushed someone through their dessert.

Harry and Marlene Brooks, owners of Hope Falls' ice cream parlor Two Scoops, enjoyed the chaotic consumption. Two Scoops was quintessential small town America with its candy striped awning outside and the white metal chairs inside. The ice cream cooler was full of all the standards and included a few dazzling options that suckered kids in with their fluorescent colors.

Beau tried to enjoy his scoop of Rocky Road, but all he could think about was his tangled up feelings for Bristol. Every time she looked at him with all the heat and the promise of pleasures to come, he lost his damn mind.

He ran through a dozen excuses for not telling her, considering and then rejecting each one. There was no getting around not telling her why he was here, why he came here looking for her.

Beau searched his memory banks for any other woman who had gotten to him like Bristol. There was no one. It wasn't just her looks, which were stunning even at six in the morning. It was her rawness, her strength. The pain of her loss had left her vulnerable, but her resolve to keep going, to keep it together, was heroic in his eyes.

He wanted her, and he suspected that having her would only be the beginning of his infatuation with Bristol. He looked up as Violet climbed into the chair opposite him. She'd abandoned her giggling crowd of friends near the front window.

"Do you like my mom?" Violet demanded over her two scoops of cookies and cream.

"What?"

She rolled her eyes with exasperation. "My mom? Tall, pretty, bossy? Do you like her?"

"I don't think I should be having this conversation with you," Beau said, skirting the issue.

Violet took a deep breath and leaned over her ice cream. "I think you should think about liking her."

"Okay. And why is that?" Beau stopped looking for an adult to rescue him from the conversation.

"She spends all her time on me or work or helping other people. But she doesn't go out and have fun. She doesn't have a boyfriend, and I think she should have one. My dad has Lissa, and he's real happy. But Mom's been so sad since Aunt Hope died."

"You think a boyfriend will make her happier?"

Violet shrugged. "She smiles a lot when she's around you, and it's been a long time since she's smiled."

The kid was stabbing him in the heart.

Violet glanced around, making sure no one else was listening in. "A couple months ago, I asked if I could spend a little more time with my dad. Since Aunt Hope's gone, Mom's all alone when I'm not there, and I thought if she had some

more time to herself she'd finally start to, like, date or something," Violet confessed.

"*That's* why you asked to spend more time with your dad?"

Violet nodded earnestly. "I don't think it's working though.
She just does more work or helps people do stuff. She babysits
for my dad and step-mom so they can go out," she leaned in.
"I'm eight, but even I know that's weird."

"Your mom is a very giving person," Beau said carefully.

"Yeah, but when's she gonna start taking? You can't just
spend your whole life giving and not taking anything for yourself, right?"

Beau stared at the dimpled cherub in her oversized hockey
jersey for a beat. "You're a really wise kid, you know that?"

"Duh." Violet sighed and settled her chin in her hands. "I
just want her to be happy. I mean she's my mom, you know?
And she's not happy."

A single, fat tear worked its way out of the corner of her
eye and slid down her cheek.

"Oh, shit—I mean shoot," Beau scrambled for the stack of
napkins on the table. "Don't do that. Don't cry."

She sniffled pitifully. "Did you ever love someone a whole
lot, and seeing them sad makes your life sad?"

He nodded. "Yeah. It sucks."

"It does suck!" Violet agreed. "So, I was thinking if you like
my mom maybe you guys could date or get married. I think
you're cool, and I think my mom does too."

"You think so?"

"She gets this big, goofy smile, and this tone like 'Beau is
so helpful'," Violet said, nailing the impression of her mother.

"I don't know, short stack," he said, spooning up the last bit
of ice cream. "I like your mom a lot, but my life is back in
Chicago."

"Can't you bring your life here?" she asked hopefully.

Hope Falls is awesome, and Grammy and Pops are here, and maybe Dad and Lissa could babysit me while you and Mom go to the movies? Or maybe I could go with you guys?"

The mind of an eight-year-old, Beau thought. *The girl was a wonder.*

"It's a lot to think about," he confessed.

Violet nodded. "I understand. You should take some time to consider and maybe get some more ice cream." She looked pointedly at where he was currently trying to scrape his spoon through the empty bowl.

Well, shit. He was head over heels for Bristol, and now he'd fallen hard for Violet. What the hell was he going to do? It wasn't like he could just pick up his life and move it here. *Could he?*

12

---

*B*eau took the B&B's porch steps two at a time and hustled through the front door. He was a man on a mission, a dangerous one.

Back at Two Scoops he'd told Bristol he needed to run a few errands before... Beau wasn't really sure what tonight was going to be. Bristol was expecting an enjoyable night of no-strings-attached sex, and Beau was going to wreck that with the truth.

Unless there was yet another Thanksgiving Eve miracle, and his apology was so moving that Bristol forgave him on the spot. If she didn't forgive him, odds were the invitation to Thanksgiving lunch wouldn't stand. But if she did, he needed to bring something. On the off chance that Bristol was incredibly forgiving, he didn't want to be "that guy" who showed up for a family holiday empty-handed.

But what the hell was he supposed to take? He was already planning on looking up "what to take to Thanksgiving" when he got back to the room.

"Whoa. You look like you're on your way to a funeral or a fire," Shelby called out from behind the front desk. She had her hair pulled back in an artsy twist and was wearing a pink apron with fluffy French poodles over her turtleneck.

He caught a glimpse of himself in the mirror above the mantel. His hair was standing out at all angles from nervously shoving his hands through it, and his eyes looked crazed. Beau stopped in his tracks. "You're a woman."

"Last time I checked," she laughed.

"I need your help."

"Color me intrigued," Shelby said, leaning over the desk and resting her chin in her hand.

"The Quinns invited me to Thanksgiving."

"The Quinns as in Bristol's family?" Shelby's eyebrows were approaching her hairline.

"Those Quinns, and I've already heard the don't drink the water or you'll get married and never leave speech from Lucky and Justin," he said, saving himself the time of another lecture on the love spell of Hope Falls.

"Well, there's always the traditional bottle of wine or flowers. You'd be fine with either of those unless, of course, you're worried about impressing them. That's a different story," she said innocently.

He waited a beat. "How different?"

"Well, you'd want to show that you put forth an effort."

"Uh-huh," he nodded. "And how would I do that?"

"How are your cooking skills?" Shelby asked.

"Grilled cheese master level."

She nodded and reached for a notebook. "I can work with that." She began scribbling on the paper. "I have this insanely easy recipe for green bean casserole. You're going to go to the store and get this stuff." She ripped off the paper and handed it over.

Beau grabbed at it like it was a million dollar lottery ticket.

"You buy the stuff, and I'll help you make it. We'll do a

double batch because I need some for tomorrow, too. While you're out, get a nice bottle of red and some kind of six-pack. Mary Quinn's side of the family is Italian, and they like their wine. Bob will appreciate the beer."

"Thank you!" Beau said fervently and ran for the door. He paused just inside the doorway. "How long does it take to make the casserole? I have... plans tonight."

From the look on her face, Beau figured Shelby knew exactly what those plans were.

"Maybe grab another bottle of wine," she suggested.

BRISTOL LUXURIATED IN A LONG, hot shower and shaved everything that needed to be smooth and moisturized everything that needed to be soft. She dried her hair and took her time reapplying some subtle, sweat proof makeup. The outfit took longer. Apparently she'd spent far too much time running a restaurant and being a parent as her wardrobe only covered those two scenarios. No sexy lingerie, no low-cut dresses. She settled for a matching bra and underwear set that were little more than a few scraps of lace, a soft scoop neck sweater that begged to be petted, and a fitted pair of capris.

If Beau had been planning to stick around town, Bristol thought she'd probably have to start investing in a more date-able wardrobe. But for tonight, this would have to do.

She felt beyond ready, and it felt damn good just to feel something. Nerves had her dusting the living room and double-checking the freshness of the sheets on the bed. She lit candles in her bedroom and immediately decided that was too over-the-top. Candlelight was more romantic wedding night than sexy fling, she decided extinguishing the flames.

With nothing left to do, Bristol decided to calm her nerves

with a little work. She settled in with her laptop at the dining room table and tackled her to do list. She fired off the last pay period's numbers to her payroll company and entered the week's expenses. A quick peek at her profit and loss statement showed that she was still comfortably up over last year. She ran a few calculations and poured herself a celebratory glass of wine when the numbers revealed that she'd have her parents and Nolan officially paid back in six months if sales continued the upswing.

She did a little victory jig in her chair. It was a solid confirmation that she was moving in the right direction. And with slow and steady growth, she could probably afford to bring in another body and buy herself an honest-to-goodness day off.

Feeling jubilant, Bristol scheduled out a week's worth of Facebook posts for Early Bird. She was just putting the finishing touches on a cute Thanksgiving graphic when her phone rang.

"If you have plans with Beau, why is he emptying the shelves of the Stop 'N Buy?" Savannah demanded.

"He's grocery shopping?"

"Canned green beans, sour cream, two of the store's most expensive bottles of wine and a crapload of other stuff. Tilly McWillis called me after he checked out. She says have fun tonight, by the way."

"Does the entire town know I'm having sex tonight?" Bristol smacked a hand to her forehead and the slap echoed around her empty loft.

"Everyone except for Dad." Savannah was not at all concerned by her sister's lack of privacy.

"Well, let's keep it that way. I'd hate for Thanksgiving at the Quinns' to end with an attempted homicide," Bristol grumbled.

Less than a minute after hanging up with Savannah, Bristol's phone was ringing again.

"Hey, Bristol," Tessa Maguire chirped.

Bristol could tell Hope Falls' favorite photographer was in her car. "Hey, Tessa. I was going to call you about your Early Bird prints after the weekend. We sold every last one of them," she said.

"Yeah? Awesome! So, I just met your Beau!" Tessa announced.

Bristol's forehead lowered to the table. "I wouldn't really call him *my* Beau."

"I would if I were you," Tessa laughed. "I ran into him when he was coming out of Grassy Meadow with two beautiful arrangements by the way. I can report via Reggie the florist that one of them is a lovely table arrangement, and the other is a dozen roses. So I'd get a vase ready if I were you."

"Thanks for the head's up, Tessa," Bristol said dryly.

"I'm swinging by the station to give my man a sloppy kiss and pick up the dog. Want me to stop by and check out your sex night outfit?"

"How about you stop by and help me pack so I can move out of this gossip mongering town?"

"Awh, poor girl. Don't be mad," Tess said affectionately. "Be happy that we all love you and want you to be happy."

"Ugh. Thanks, Tessa."

"Wishing you many orgasms," she said cheerily before disconnecting.

BEAU WEDGED his foot in the door next to Early Bird and shouldered his way through. When he'd returned to the B&B

with his beast of burden-sized load, Shelby's jaw had hit the floor. "I guess you really want to impress, huh?"

To be honest, it had been fun to shop. His condo had been fully stocked by a housekeeper and a personal chef. After that, there'd been so much time spent in hospitals eating out of vending machines and fluorescent-lit cafeterias that he hadn't stepped foot in a grocery store, preferring to order delivery whenever he and Alli were home.

He'd made two batches of Shelby's grandma's green bean casserole in the B&B's kitchen, showered as quickly as possible without missing anything important, and loaded everything he'd need for every contingency into his truck.

There were flowers and wine for seduction or apology, food and snacks in case they decided to just talk, and an overnight bag and condoms—that he'd driven to neighboring Longview to buy—in case everything went really well.

He wrestled the load up the stairs and was debating whether to kick at the door or put everything down and knock like a gentleman when it flew open.

Bristol was wearing cropped pants that hugged her long, long legs. Her sweater, a cornflower blue, dipped low at her breasts. She wore her hair long and loose, tempting his fingers to drop their load and dive into those rich tresses.

"You're the most beautiful woman I've ever seen," he breathed. He hadn't meant for the words to come out, but his honesty was rewarded when Bristol launched herself at him. He dropped the bags to catch her, grabbing her by the hips and lifting her. She wrapped her arms and legs around him, her lips fusing to his.

He lost the power of independent thought when her mouth opened, and she invited him in with a breathy whimper. Beau poured himself into the kiss. It wasn't purely selfish. He wanted to give her this, the undeniable evidence of his feelings for her so that no matter what happened tonight, she could remember this moment and know.

He cared for her. He *ached* for her. But he owed her the truth.

"Bristol, wait." He tried pulling back, but she followed him and their mouths tangled again. "Wait, gorgeous. There's something I have to tell you."

She unwrapped those long, perfect legs from his waist and slid down his body. He groaned at the friction of her sliding over his erection. She responded by nipping at his lower lip.

"You're not married are you?" she demanded, her blue eyes narrowing.

"God, no!"

She kissed him senseless again, a reward for being unmarried. "Seeing someone?"

"No," he breathed, trying desperately to hang on to his train of thought.

"Good. Killed anyone?" Bristol licked the seam of his lips, and his cock strained painfully against his zipper.

"Huh-uh," he shook his head.

"Any STDs?"

"Jesus, Bristol! No. I'm clean."

Good to know. I think that covers it."

"Bristol—"

"Beau." She trailed a finger down his sweater over his chest and down across his taut abs to the waistband of his jeans. "I'm not overly familiar with fling protocol, but since we're looking at one beautiful night of obscene pleasure instead of years of commitment, I don't think there's anything you need to confess right now."

She dipped her fingers into the denim, and his dick flexed painfully in anticipation. He was losing the battle.

Beau closed his eyes as she released the button of his fly. "Are you sure?" he whispered, already hating himself.

"You're a good man. I believe that with all my heart. And that's what matters most to me. Okay?"

He'd make it up to her. No matter what it took, he would fix it.

"Okay," he said, in a low whisper. She lowered his zipper, and Beau put his hands on her and turned off his mind.

13

———

*B*ristol could tell the second Beau gave up fighting the good guy fight. His hands were suddenly everywhere, tangling in her hair, cruising her waist, snaking behind her to grab a handful of round, firm flesh.

Their kiss became more frantic as they dove into the exploration of their bodies. With Beau's jeans already open, Bristol slid her hands under his shirt and worked it over his head.

"Oh, holy hell you're built," she whispered, raining kisses over each perfectly formed pec. He had the torso of a Greek god, ripped and powerful.

"Mmm," he groaned, shoving her back against her open front door, pinning her in place to yank her sweater over her head. "You, too."

He drove his wide palms over the satin and lace of her bra and squeezed. Her blood sang as she sagged against him, pinned between the heavy wood of her door and Beau's rock hard body.

"God, you're perfect," he groaned, keeping one hand on a breast while working the zipper on her pants with the other.

Bristol shoved her hand into his jeans and confirmed that he was, in fact, an Adonis everywhere. She cupped the rigid length of his hard-on through his silky soft briefs. "I need you out of these jeans like yesterday."

She murmured the words, but he shucked the pants and kicked them down the hallway as if she'd threatened him.

"Jesus, do you live in a gym?" Bristol stroked over every rippled ab. Every inch of him was built. His shoulders and chest were broad and muscled. Those spectacular abs went beyond six-pack, and his thighs were thick and oh so hard.

His arms wrapped around her like steel bands. Every inch of him was scorching hot and hard as marble.

Beau's beard tickled her neck as he let his mouth devour the sensitive flesh he found there. She shoved her hand into the sexy navy briefs and gripped his shaft. He shuddered against her as a noise, primal and pained, rose from his chest. She relished the effect she had on him, stroking his cock from root to tip.

Moisture leaked from the head, slicking her hand. Beau blew out a breath and gripped her shoulders. "Bristol, baby, are you sure?"

"Haven't I made it clear enough?" Her words were breathless, and she stroked him again, this time a little rougher.

"I want to know what you want, what you like. How I can —" He sucked in a breath as she pumped him harder.

"Beau, I want you. And I have no problem telling you what I want as we go."

"Be sure, baby."

His concern with what she wanted was even sexier than if he'd just ripped off her clothes and sank into her. "I'm sure. I want you right here, Beau."

She could have shot him and gotten less of a reaction. One second, he was looming over her letting her tease his aching dick, and the next, he was pushing her into the apartment and dragging his discarded bags inside. He slammed the door and locked it behind him.

He looked like a fallen angel, she thought, a determined one as he stalked toward her, the head of his engorged penis erupting out of the top of his briefs.

She'd never seen anything sexier in her entire life, and the visual did nothing to calm the frantic throb she felt between her legs. He tossed a box of condoms on the floor next to her and dove.

Bristol wasn't sure how she ended up on the floor, but she didn't care once the heat and weight of Beau's body covered her. He rained kisses and bites down on her neck and shoulders, nudging the purple bra straps down her arms.

His lips skimmed over the upper curves of her breasts that were desperately trying to escape the lingerie she'd imprisoned them in.

Beau dipped his tongue under the lace edge, and Bristol felt a lightning bolt snake through her when the tip skimmed over her pebbled nipple.

"Beau!" She gasped out his name, arching her back and urging him to take more.

She saw his hand shake when he reached for the front clasp of her bra and grabbed it, stopping him. "Are you sure? Do you want me?" she asked him.

"Gorgeous, there is nothing in this universe that I have ever wanted more than you. I just don't want to fuck this up."

His sweetness gave another little jumpstart to her heart. She'd wanted this to be a wild fling, but Beau was finding ways to make her feel treasured, worshipped. She brought her hand up to cup his face. "I won't let you," she promised.

"I'm holding you to that." He brushed a wave of glossy

chestnut hair away from her face. "Fling or no fling, you matter to me, Bristol." His voice was gruff.

"Then show me, Beau." She unhooked her bra and offered herself to him.

He showed her with every kiss, every caress, every scrape of his teeth. The stiff bristles of his beard abraded the soft flesh of her breasts as he kissed, sampled, and sucked.

Her bare heels dug into the hardwood beneath her as he devoured. He made her feel... everything. The emotions that had hibernated within her came to life under Beau's masterful attention. He released her breasts to work his way down the flat of her stomach, and when his fingers stopped at the waistband of her pants, Bristol levered up so he could work them free.

Her carefully chosen thong was admired by Beau's heated green gaze for nearly a full second before he was dragging it down her legs.

"It's not enough," Beau whispered reverently, his breath hot on her thigh.

"What's not?"

"One night."

Her heart wept at the tender words.

He stroked a hand up her thigh, and Bristol's hips jacked up from the floor when he skimmed blunt fingertips over bare flesh.

"We'll have to make the most of it," she gasped.

"Open for me, gorgeous."

She let her knees fall open to the sides and threaded her fingers through his free hand while he gently parted her already wet folds with his other. She felt his erection throb against her thigh, and when he slid two long fingers into her center, she sighed out his name.

"God, you're so ready for me," Beau whispered. He leaned

in and down and traced his tongue over her folds. The breath in Bristol's lungs exploded out in a hiss.

"Is this okay?" he asked.

"Only if your goal is to murder me with pleasure, and at this point, go right ahead."

Beau's soft laugh was lost when he dipped his head to taste her again. His tongue laved that delicate bundle of nerves while his fingers drove her higher. Over and over, he lapped and licked at her and when she felt herself sliding toward the edge, her muscles already quivering, she grabbed his wrist.

"Beau, stop. You're going to make me come," she whispered desperately.

"I'm not seeing a problem," he said, placing a gentle kiss on the inside of her thigh.

"I want your cock inside me the first time you make me come."

Beau froze as if trying to understand what language she was speaking. Judging from the amount of fluid leaking from the crown of his penis, that part had caught up faster than his brain. She took matters into her own hands, pushing him down on the hard floor, and when she swiveled, when he understood her intent, Beau growled his approval.

She lay opposite him on her side, facing his throbbing erection. She felt his hands on her, gently opening her legs. His breath was hot against her, and she knew he would force her over the edge, but she was determined to take him with her.

Impatiently, she shoved his briefs down those spectacular thighs, freeing his achingly hard cock. Without preamble, she gripped it by the base and brought her wet mouth to the crown. When her lips parted, flowing down the solid column of flesh, he bucked reflexively against her, forcing himself further down her throat.

Beau's grip tightened on her inner thigh to the point of pain. He dove into her, stroking and teasing with his tongue. Again, he eased his fingers into her. He followed the brutal pace she set.

She hummed her approval with his hard-on deep in her throat, and she heard his low rumble in return.

They were animals for each other, giving in to the ages-old drive to mate. He was making her mad, shredding every boundary, drowning her in sensation even as he fought against the pleasure she sought to give him.

"Bristol, baby, slow down," he ordered. The easy-going man she'd fallen for was gone, and in his place was one hell bent on torturing her with a pleasure so excruciating Bristol knew she'd never recover.

She had no intention of slowing down. She wanted him as hot and as frantic as he made her, and she wanted to taste him. But just then, the long jagged peak she'd been sprinting up dropped out from under her. The orgasm detonated in her core and radiated outward in waves of ecstasy. She could only moan around his thick member as her release leveled her.

He tasted her as she came, holding her still when she would have pulled away. Beau steadied her, worshipped her, until the last of the quaking subsided.

"There's no way I can do that again," she gasped, nuzzling his cock.

"Oh, gorgeous, you are so wrong." She could hear the cocky smile in his voice just before the sound of cardboard shredding. Bristol managed to pry open one eye to see Beau tearing open the box of condoms. Seeing his desperation to have her ratcheted up her own need. He hadn't even touched her again, and she was already halfway there. She watched him slick on a condom and prime himself with his hand. The empty ache between her legs was suddenly unbearable. Her body was begging for him.

"Here?" he asked.

"God, yes, Beau. Here."

And then he was ranging himself over her. She felt him hard and hungry prodding her center. "Yes," she whispered her plea. And then he was easing into her. The pressure, the fullness, shocked her when he sank into her, and his cry of victory had her clenching around him.

"Relax for me, baby," he demanded, his beard tickling the skin under her ear.

When she did, slowly, purposefully, the last inch of his cock slid into her.

His groan was another aphrodisiac. Testing, he carefully pulled out before lazily sliding back home. Beau was moving with care, but Bristol could feel his body demanding more. The need vibrated under his sweat-slicked skin. She bit into his shoulder and tasted the salt.

He sank into her again, a little faster, a little more desperately, and buried his face in her neck. Bristol let the flood of sensation carry her away. Ignoring the bite of the floor, her hips rose to meet his powerful thrusts. His chest hair tickled her and the muscles bunched under her fingers.

Now, she knew he was right. She could go up again. She was practically there already.

"Hold onto me, gorgeous," he murmured, and when her arms locked around his shoulders, he pulled her up. Still joined, she found herself straddling Beau, his back against the wall. "I need to see you."

Sex had never been this intimate before, Bristol thought as her eyes locked with his. Not wanting to lose their momentum, she used her thighs to rise up before sinking down on him. They sighed together over that pleasure, and Bristol picked her pace. Beau's arms held her locked tight in place against him so that her nipples brushed his chest as she rode him.

She was so full inside, so hot. It was as if making love to Beau had unleashed the feelings that had been locked up for so long.

It was beautiful, it was painful, it was cathartic.

Bristol rode faster, and when those longer fingers dug into her flesh, she knew she was carrying him past his limits. They breathed together, the same steamy air.

Those gorgeous green eyes glazed over in front of her, and Bristol felt powerful. The delicate muscles in her channel began to quiver.

God, it was happening again.

"Beau?" His name was a question on her lips.

"I've got you, baby. I'm yours," he gritted out the words, and the first flutter of her release set him off. He jerked inside her, the cords of his neck taut with the effort. She was coming fast and hard with him. Wrapped around each other, they shattered from the inside out with the wild pumps of his cock controlling her own brutal orgasm.

"Bristol," he whispered her name over and over again into her neck until he was finally empty.

14

Minutes or possibly hours later, Beau gathered her up in his arms and carried her to the bedroom. He placed her gently on the thick-striped comforter of the bed.

He'd been emptied and left raw and satisfied. Judging from the smug smile that hovered on those rosy lips, Bristol felt the same.

He sat next to her, against the upholstered headboard and mountain of pillows, and brushed her hair back from her face. "Bristol?"

"Mmm?"

"How do you feel?"

She didn't open her eyes, but her smile bloomed smug and satisfied, her dimples winking to life. "Good. Sleepy. Hungry."

"I brought dinner."

"In the bags you threw on the stairs when I jumped you?"

"It's frozen pizza," he said. "I'm sure it's fine."

"Mmm, pizza," she yawned. "Let's eat and then do that again."

He gave in to the urge and stroked his fingers through that glossy brown curtain of hair. "You liked it?" he asked.

The pillow hit him in the face. "Now I know you can't seriously be asking because you don't recognize earth-moving, body-shattering sex when you have it."

"Just looking for a verbal confirmation that it was a mutually satisfying experience," he grinned.

"Oh, and me screaming your name was too subtle?"

"I've never heard anything better in my entire life." Beau's life had just changed, and he wasn't about to pretend to deny it. His entire world was in Chicago and on hold. And the woman who had single-handedly changed all that thought he was someone else.

He could fix this, somehow. He just needed a little more time to figure things out.

"You look phenomenal naked," Bristol announced. "Does yoga really do all that?" She waved a hand at his torso.

"How about you stay here, and I'll make the pizza?" he offered, ignoring her question.

She curled on her side, hugging a pillow to her spectacular chest. "Mmm, 'k."

Beau dropped a kiss on her forehead and then one on her lips, which went further than he intended. By the time he broke away and escaped, he was hard as stone again and couldn't zip his jeans.

When he returned minutes later, he found Bristol in much the same position he'd left her in except for the fact that she was guiltily shoving her phone under her pillow.

He handed her a glass of wine and put his on the nightstand. There he found the matches, and he worked his way around the room lighting the clusters of candles she'd placed everywhere.

"So of the entire population of Hope Falls, what percentage is aware of what we just did?" he asked.

"The night is young, so probably only fifty to fifty-five percent," she guessed. "And I swear, I was mostly just checking on Violet—she's making pumpkin roll with Grammy, by the way. I wasn't gloating about our dirty deeds. Except to Vanna and Lissa."

"Are your parents going to want me in their house tomorrow after word spreads?" he asked, sliding onto the bed next to her and pulling her into his side.

She propped herself on his chest. "Relax, Beau. Hope Falls may be nosey, but we know enough not to tell people things they don't need to know. Besides, I think they're looking forward to a new plus one. It'll help take everyone's minds off of Hope."

The name of the woman who had brought him here had him tensing. "If there's anything I can do to help, Bristol, please let me know."

She gave him a sad smile. "Thanks, Beau. I feel bad for you walking into this. We're a wounded family. All those traditions we established over the years, every single one of them was built on the whole. But we're not whole anymore."

She stared into her glass of wine. "We're missing so many puzzle pieces. Hope was the one who insisted we wear pajamas for Thanksgiving. Every Christmas Eve, she and Violet made the cookies for Santa. There are so many holes where she should be. I think the whole town is going to feel it. She always helped organize the Christmas Eve Carnival."

"You have a carnival on Christmas Eve?" Beau asked, picking up his glass of wine.

"That's what all the outsiders say until they go to one," Bristol joked. "Every year on Christmas Eve, the whole town turns out at Riverside Park for hot chocolate and carols and a walk through the lights. There's a pie contest, too. It's just a small town way of taking a break from the chaos so we can all really enjoy the holiday, the community."

"It sounds nice," he admitted.

"It is. And every year, Hope was there, doling out hot chocolate, organizing the choir, judging the Santa contest. But not this year."

"I'm sorry, Bristol."

She sighed heavily. "I've been thinking about her a lot lately. Everything seems to remind me of her. You know the building next door?"

The building next to Early Bird was an exact replica of its three-story brick neighbor.

"Yeah, the hardware store. Mr. Maybry, the out-of-work handy man."

Bristol nodded. "Good memory. Pollard's. They'd been in business for sixty-plus years, and when Mr. Pollard Jr. died, Hope wanted to buy the building and keep the retail downstairs and do lofts on the top two floors. 'We'd be neighbors for life,' she'd say."

"And you can't help but think of that every time you walk outside," Beau predicted.

"All the 'what might have beens' are really crushing my holiday spirit." She shook her head. "I'm sorry. I don't know where all of that came from. I seem to dump sad on you every time we're together. Let's forget I totally brought the mood down."

He stroked her hair again. "Bristol, you don't have to pretend everything's okay with me. I don't need you to be strong for me."

She looked up at him, her brow furrowed. "You see a lot with those sexy green eyes."

"I hope to see a lot more before the end of the night."

They ate pizza and made love—several more times—and laughed and slept. And when he woke in the morning, with Bristol still in his arms, Beau knew there was no going back. He was in love with Bristol Quinn, and he wasn't letting go.

❧

"ARE you sure it's okay that I'm here?" Beau asked for the third time since getting out of Bristol's car in front of Bristol's parents' house. They lived in a cozy brick bungalow on a corner lot. There was a wreath on the door and an inflatable Santa on the tiny patch of lawn.

"Beau, you brought enough food and booze to feed an army. My mom's going to be impressed, and my Dad is just happy you have a penis," Bristol said, her chin holding the top casserole dish in place.

"What about the pajamas? Does everyone really wear pajamas, or are you punking me?" he asked, looking down at his flannel pajama pants.

"Beau, trust me," Bristol grinned. "Everything is going to be fine. Now, are you ready for chaos?"

Beau swallowed hard. He'd faced disappointed fans, aggressive reporters, and jacked up opponents. He could do this. "Let's do this."

Bristol gave the front door a well-placed kick, and it swung open. It sounded to Beau like there were a thousand angry people inside.

"Remember that my mom's Italian?" Bristol shouted over her shoulder at him.

"Yeah."

"Well, so are her sister, her aunt, and her mother."

He followed her through the foyer, past the living room

crowded with furniture, and down the skinny hallway toward the chatter and the scents of turkey and gravy.

He watched her disappear into the kitchen and heard the chorus of greetings.

"There she is!"

"Doesn't she look beautiful?"

"I hope you made those sweet potatoes!"

"Hi, Nana! Aunt Cara, Aunt Lia, you're looking beautiful as always," Bristol's greetings rang out.

When he stepped into the kitchen, just one foot on the green linoleum, a hush fell over the room. It was a small kitchen, but they'd managed to squeeze in the entire female population of the family. The windows were steamed up from all the cooking and body heat, and everyone was wielding wine glasses.

Lissa and Savannah, thankfully in colorful pajama leggings and sweatshirts, looked up from the mountain of potatoes they were peeling at the small table. They waved and smiled as if they knew exactly how he'd spent the last eighteen hours of his life.

Mary, in a pair of pink pajama bottoms covered in kittens, shoved a glass of wine at Bristol and directed Violet in the potato mashing department. Bristol gave her daughter a kiss on the top of the head and admired her potato handiwork.

But the other three women with their dark hair and eyes like Mary's watched him warily. He felt as though he'd just stepped into the lioness's den.

"Everybody, this is Beau," Bristol said, making the introduction. "Beau, this is everyone. My nana, Ludavine." The woman dressed in head-to-toe black nodded imperiously. Her graying hair was cut in a sleek bob, and though she had to be hovering around seventy, her face was mostly unlined. "This is my Great-Aunt Cara," Bristol continued, pointing at the woman in plain flannel pajamas sitting on the barstool and stirring the pot on the stove that bubbled. "And my Aunt Lia." Lia, a carbon copy of Mary, in pink puppy pants, smiled cheerfully.

"Hi, Beau," they said as one.

"Hi, everyone. Thank you for inviting me, Mrs. Quinn," he said, handing over the fall-themed centerpiece he'd gotten her.

They all began speaking at once, but to whom and about what he couldn't tell. Lia grabbed the bags out of his hands and started unloading. The bottle of wine went straight to the corkscrew, he noted.

When Lia returned, it was with the six-pack she'd dug out of the shopping bag. "Okay, you're going to take this, and you're going to go outside to the garage. Take your coat, too."

Not sure if he'd just been kicked out or given a reprieve, Beau trudged back down the hallway, the sounds of female chatter seeming only to get louder behind him.

He let himself out the front door and wandered around the side of the house. At the back of the lot was a one-car garage in the same brick as the house. When he peered through the glass of the door, he spotted salvation.

Big Bob Quinn himself in fleece plaid pants waved Beau inside and became even more cheerful when he spotted the six-pack. "Thank God. You just saved us a trip back into that she den."

"Us" consisted of Nolan, Bristol's affable ex, and a tall, skinny guy hunched over the rabbit-eared thirteen-inch TV shouting profanity at a referee who couldn't hear him.

"Glad I could help." He should have gotten a case.

"Grab a chair," Bob said, helping himself to one of the beers.

"Hey, I'm Vince, Savanna's fiancé," the skinny guy said,

offering his hand when he was done yelling.

"Vince, nice to meet you. I'm Beau."

"Crazy in there isn't it?" Nolan said, pulling up an extra camp chair for Beau and grabbing a beer out of the pack.

"I've never seen anything like it."

"You ever see that movie *My Big Fat Greek Wedding*?" Vince asked.

Beau shook his head. He had. Alli had made the entire team watch it on a road trip once, but he wasn't about to admit that. "No, but I know the gist of it."

"This is like My Big Fat Italian Thanksgiving," Bob said, chugging the beer as if it were medicinal.

Beau sat back in his chair, popped the top on a beer, and finally started to relax.

THE RELAXATION CAME to a screeching halt when Violet came to collect them. The men were welcomed back into the house by a slightly tipsier group of women than he'd left. They all crowded around the table in the Quinns' tiny dining room. Violet and Bristol had to crawl under the table that had been extended to its full length to accommodate the crowd just to reach their seats in the corner.

Beau took a seat next to Bristol. There was a box of tissues in front of his plate. In fact there were three boxes of tissues on the table.

Once they were all seated Nana Ludavine cleared her throat, and everyone quieted. Ready for whatever grace the Quinns said, Beau bowed his head.

"Okay the rules are everybody passes the food unless your arms are broken, and everybody tries a bite of everything with no whining," she looked fiercely at Violet who smiled. "And no crying. Anyone starts to cry, we change the subject. We have a lot to be thankful for, and that's what we should be thinking about today."

Beau looked around the table to gauge the reaction to Ludavine's laws. Since the food was already being passed, he assumed all had accepted the edicts. Bristol squeezed his thigh under the table. "How'd it go in Man Land?" she whispered.

"Very peaceful," he said, heaping potatoes onto both their plates from the bottomless bowl that Mary helpfully shoved at him.

Nolan and Lissa sat at the foot of the table crammed against the bay window. Lyric smeared potatoes and corn into a pattern on the tray of her highchair. Vince caught Beau's attention and mimed drinking. Beau nodded vigorously. From a cooler at his feet, Savannah's fiancé produced four cans of light beer and tossed them around the table.

"Who's sitting at that place?" Violet asked through a mouthful of stuffing. She pointed down to the empty place setting on the opposite end of the table next to Great-Aunt Cara. Beau saw Mary's hand tremble when she reached for her wine glass.

"That's for Aunt Hope," Bristol explained quietly.

"But she's not here anymore," Violet pressed, confusion written on her pretty little face.

"We don't want to forget Aunt Hope," Bristol said, her voice thickening with emotion. "We want to feel like part of her is still here with us."

Beau reached under the table and squeezed her leg. They all heard the whimper, and Beau looked on in horror as Lissa's face crumpled, and she reached for her napkin.

"Oh, crap," Bob muttered, his eyes watering. "Lissa, you hang in there, you hear me?"

Someone else sniffled.

"Subject change!" Vince announced at a near shout. "Mary, this turkey is delicious. Is it free range?"

"What does free range mean?" Ludavine demanded.

Lissa put her napkin down and took a large gulp of wine. Aunt Lia passed the bottle around.

He admired them all. Their determination to stay grateful to enjoy their time together, even when the absence of one was so painful, was a testament to the strength of their family. They protected their own, just as he would. He respected that.

They chattered on, Beau deflecting questions about yoga and Bristol deflecting questions about marriage. They stumbled a few times but managed to make it to dessert without breaking any of the rules.

Mary and Lia got up to bring the desserts in despite the fact that no one at the table had any room for more.

When Mary placed Bristol's pecan pie on the table another silence descended. "Is that...?" Savannah asked, not wanting to finish the question.

Bristol nodded. "Yeah. I found her recipe." She wiped at her eye.

"It's a good pie, not a reason to be sad," Nana Ludavine said, dabbing the corners of her eyes with the napkin.

Beau looked down at the pie. In the very center was a small heart. He felt his throat start to tighten. Mary trembled next to him, trying to hold back a flood of emotions. He put one hand on Bristol's leg and patted Mary's shoulder awkwardly with the other. The aunts were sniffling, and Bob was blowing his nose. Nolan, his own eyes damp, wiped a tear from Violet's cheek.

"Subject change!" Beau announced in desperation. "Who wants another drink?"

"Me!" Everyone including Violet wanted one.

"Can I have a soda?" Violet asked.

"Kid, you can have anything you want," Beau said, and everyone laughed. They opened another bottle of wine, and Bob grabbed another round of beers out of the refrigerator and doled them out. He looked around the table, eyes still misty and raised his beer. "Look, I know we're all missing our Hope. It's a hard day for all of us, being reminded of what we lost. I'd just like to thank you all for being here and for making this day as special as it can be."

No one was bothering to try to hide it now. Beau grabbed a fistful of tissues and handed half to Mary and half to Bristol. *He shouldn't be here,* he realized. They should be able to grieve in peace. Coming here had been a mistake. They weren't ready, and maybe neither was he.

"I'd also like to thank Bristol," Bob continued. She looked up to meet her father's red eyes. "You helped us make the decision to donate Hope's organs. Without you speaking up when you did, I don't think we would have had the guts to do it. And now, knowing that pieces of her are living on in others is what gives us the greatest comfort."

Bristol stifled a sob, and Beau unfroze from his seat long enough to slide a comforting arm around her shoulders. He had her to thank. She had saved the only thing in this world that had mattered to him... until now. *She was his hero.*

The guests around the table blew their noses and raised their glasses and cans.

"To Hope," Bob said, laying a hand on his wife's shoulder.

"To Hope," everyone echoed.

To Hope, Beau repeated in his head. *I promise you, Hope, I will make things right for your family.*

A sad silence settled in the room, and no one seemed willing to change the subject this time.

"Hey, who likes puppies?" Violet piped up.

15

*B*ristol woke early. It was still dark, her body still blissfully used and sore from another night with Beau. They'd waved Violet off with Nolan and Lissa on their annual road trip to Lissa's family in Monterey. And Beau had given her an extra hard hug when she'd cried.

But he'd taken her home, taken her straight to bed where they'd napped for two hours. And when they woke, there was no more napping.

Physically their bodies were so in tune. He knew everything she wanted from him without her ever voicing it. And it wasn't just in the bed—or on the floor or the kitchen island.

He'd been a rock for her entire family yesterday, supporting them with humor and sweetness and, in the end, some impressive bartending skills. Even Nana had approved. She'd given Bristol a good hard look on her way out the door and nodded in Beau's direction.

"He's a good man. You let him marry you," she'd insisted.

Bristol smiled at the memory. He was a good man, and she'd had more than a few not-so-fleeting wishes that he'd stay in the past twenty-four hours. Even longer, if she was being completely honest.

She let herself daydream for just a second. Beau in Hope Falls, Beau coaching Violet's hockey team, Beau in her kitchen, her bedroom... *their* kitchen, *their* bedroom.

She rolled over, reaching for him, but found his side of the bed empty. A glance at the clock told her she still had fifteen minutes before she had to get up for the anarchy of Black Friday at Early Bird. It wasn't that it was a big shopping day in Hope Falls, Bristol thought as she pulled on Beau's discarded t-shirt. It was that everyone had just spent the last twenty-four hours cooking, cleaning, and entertaining family. It was time to get out of the house.

She padded out to the kitchen and found it dark. She felt the tickle of worry in her belly when she walked to the front window. It was snowing steadily. Beau's SUV had been parked in front of her car. It was gone.

She hurried back to the kitchen, desperate for caffeine to help her make sense of it all. *Had she dreamed it? Had he told her he wasn't staying the night?*

She flicked on the lights over the island and was reaching for the coffee maker when a piece of paper caught her eye. It was propped up against the vase holding the slightly squished roses he'd given her.

Gorgeous,

I owe you an explanation for why I came and why I left, but I can't. Not yet. These last few days have changed everything for me. You've changed everything for me. Well, you, Violet, your family, hell, even the rest of this crazy town. I'll be back. I prom-

ise, and I'll explain everything. I hope you can forgive me for lying.

Love,
*   Beau*

~

THE SNOW DIDN'T SCARE anyone off of breakfast. Not in a town that was walkable end to end in twenty minutes. Early Bird was at full capacity by seven-thirty. The coffee was strong and the windows were steaming up as plates of eggs and sausage and pancakes rotated with the crowd.

But gone was Bristol's post-sex buzz. Gone were her daydreams of Beau in Hope Falls. And gone was her heart.

He'd lied to her, slept with her, and left her. And he was going to pay.

"Take a break."

Her sister's voice snapped Bristol out of her revenge fantasy.

"What are you doing here?" Bristol frowned.

She saw her sister skate a look at Margo who whistled innocently as she turned around and slunk back to the kitchen.

"I see."

"Grab a mug and take five and tell me why you don't have orgasmic bliss written all over your face. And I want an egg white omelet with turkey bacon and coffee."

Bristol glared at her sister while she rang in the order and snatched two mugs off the wall.

Savannah snagged a table as it was abandoned by Mr. King and aging hippie Art Gardine. "So talk."

"Beau's gone."

"What the hell do you mean he's gone? He was slobbering over you yesterday. Lissa used the 'L' word," Savannah argued.

"What? Lust?" Bristol snorted. "Loser?" She was so mad she couldn't come up with any other 'L' words.

"What happened when you went home yesterday?" Savannah asked, determined to get to the bottom of it.

"We took a nap."

"Is that a euphemism?" Savannah frowned.

"No! We fell asleep all snuggled up together like an idiot and a liar and then when we woke up we... did other things that occur in beds. We ate the leftovers Mom packed up for us and then went back to bed for more..."

"Occurrences," Savannah provided.

"And when I woke up at four, he was gone, and this was in the kitchen."

She yanked the note out of her pocket and slapped it on the table.

Savannah snatched it up, read it. "What the fuck is this?"

"I would really like to know!"

"You changed everything, but he can't explain why he was lying or leaving?" Savannah reiterated. "We're getting to the bottom of this, and then we're driving to Chicago—if that is where he's from— and setting his house on fire."

"Thanks for having my back."

"No one messes with my sister. Not even someone who looks like Beau French."

"If that's his real name."

~

SAVANNAH AND BRISTOL agreed to meet at Bristol's that afternoon for some cyber stalking, but first, there was one thing Bristol needed to do.

She drove out to Mountain Meadow B&B in the still falling snow. She already knew Beau wouldn't be there, but maybe Shelby or Levi could shed some light on the man's mysterious disappearance.

"Hey, Bristol! How'd you fare in the snow?" Shelby asked with a warm grin. She was on a ladder decorating the B&B's Christmas tree.

"Uh, good. Everything was fine. You?"

"Levi had the paths and sidewalks cleared in no time. We ended up with a good crowd at JT's last night despite the snow. Everyone hiked in on snowshoes," Shelby laughed. Shelby was a San Diego native and was still adjusting to the culture shock of Hope Falls. "So what can I do for you?"

"I was wondering if Beau French was still here?"

Shelby frowned down at her. "You mean Beau Evanko?"

Bristol shook her head. "French. He was here for the yoga retreat," Bristol tried again.

"We had a Beau Evanko, and I believe he was the very attractive man who went to Thanksgiving lunch with you. He made the green bean casserole here."

Bristol felt a sick feeling of dread slide through her stomach.

Shelby climbed down the ladder. "What's wrong? You look like you're going to be sick."

Bristol reached into her bag and dug for her phone. "Is this Beau Evanko?" she asked, pulling up a picture on her phone.

Shelby leaned in to look. "Yep, that's him." She pulled back to study Bristol. "He left his room key at the desk overnight. I found it this morning."

With a heavy heart, Bristol shoved her phone back in her bag.

"There's no way that guy is a yoga instructor. He told me

he was here to visit a family connection. Come to think of it, he was super vague about it, but I never was able to weasel out of him who it was."

"He worked out at Lucky's once or twice," Bristol tried again. "Do you think Lucky or Levi know anything about him?"

"If Levi knows anything about Beau and didn't tell me, he's going to be sleeping on the couch tonight," Shelby threatened. "He really told you his name was French and that he was a yoga instructor?"

Bristol nodded already feeling like a prize idiot.

"He seemed really nice, sweet even. He was so nervous about Thanksgiving with your family. Why would he do that to you?"

Bristol took a deep breath. "I don't know, but I'm going to find out."

"If he shows his face here again, you can bet I'll be dialing you while Levi beats the hell out of him," Shelby said, angry now.

"Thanks, Shelby. I appreciate it."

~

"HE'S A PROFESSIONAL HOCKEY PLAYER?" Bristol screeched.

"Was," Savannah corrected her, squinting at her laptop screen. "This says he retired suddenly about a year ago."

"Why? Was he caught embezzling from the PHL? Did he sleep with the team captain and then disappear off the face of the earth?" Bristol snapped.

Savannah shook her head. "He was the team captain. The official statement says 'personal reasons.' Lots of speculation, but he never went public with his reason for leaving the sport." She wiggled her empty wine glass at Bristol. "Need more stalking fuel."

Bristol took the glass into the kitchen and opened a new bottle of wine while Savannah clicked and scrolled some more. Today had been the single biggest day in Early Bird's history. She should be celebrating. Instead, she was pacing her apartment trying to unmask the man who had brought her back to life and then discarded her like the unwanted bottom of a muffin.

"Holy effing shit."

"What?" Bristol asked, practically climbing over her sister's shoulder to see the screen. "Is he under investigation for murder? Oh, my God," she gasped. "Is he *married*?"

Savannah swiveled around to look at her. "Why would married get a bigger reaction out of you than murdering?"

"I don't know!" Bristol said as she paced back and forth behind her chair. "I just—shut up and tell me if he has a criminal record, okay?"

"News today out of Chicago says that Beau Evanko just put his swanky downtown penthouse on the market for a cool $2.5 million."

Bristol handed Savannah the full glass and took a sip of her own.

"We're missing something here. Why would a professional hockey player fly out here, pretend to be a yoga instructor, seduce me, and then vanish again?"

Savannah rolled her shoulders. "We've got to be missing something. Some connection. Maybe he's looking for something to do with his millions, and he wants to franchise Early Bird?"

"Maybe he's an asshole who gets off on seducing single moms and then disappearing on them." Bristol flopped down in one of the dining chairs. "I really liked him. Like really liked him."

Savannah covered her hand. "B, we all did. That couldn't have been an act, not all of it. He's a hockey player, not a member of the Screen Actors Guild."

Bristol dropped her forehead to the table. "I feel like such an idiot. I trusted him. I let him be around Violet!" She thunked her head once. "The other team parents are going to kill me! How could I have let a stranger coach those kids?"

"No one in Hope Falls has ever been strung up for falling in love."

"Love? This isn't love!" Bristol sat upright. "Even if I was feeling something similar to love, it was *not* real love because real love is based on honesty, not lies some really hot asshole tells to get laid."

"Something is not adding up here," Savannah said, not even pretending to listen to Bristol's tirade. "He's totally hot. He wouldn't have to lie to get anyone in bed. There has to be a reason why Beau Evanko came to Hope Falls."

It flashed into her mind, Beau's words two nights ago before...

"Wait, gorgeous. There's something I have to tell you."

In the heat of the moment, he'd tried to tell her something. He'd tried to stop her, and she'd told him it wasn't important. It could wait.

"What? What's wrong?" Savannah demanded. "You look like you smell something bad."

~

THE DAYS PASSED SWIFTLY thanks to Violet coming home with stories to tell of Monterey and the last minute wedding preparations. But always in the back of her mind was Beau Evanko.

At night, when Violet was in bed, Bristol dug deeper into the man she'd thought she'd known. She'd seen every highlight of his career thanks to an Evanko Fans channel on YouTube. Even with her limited knowledge of the sport, she could tell he'd been an incredible player. He was an MVP god on skates.

There were hundreds of pictures of Beau handing out signed jerseys to kids at games or signing autographs. He'd visited children's hospitals in full uniform. He'd donated hundreds of thousands of dollars to several worthwhile charities. There was even a freaking Beau Evanko doll with matching kid-sized jersey from which all proceeds went to a children's charity.

So he was generous, Bristol had mused cynically. *That didn't mean he wasn't a generous asshole.*

She'd also spent hours tracking down every single picture of every woman Beau had escorted anywhere. In the past several years, it had been the same five blondes recycled for public appearances. Interestingly enough, each blonde was labeled the sister or cousin of a different Chicago Wind player. She couldn't imagine the scenario where a guy wouldn't mind his little sis being one of five girlfriends.

Speaking of little sisters, there were a handful of pictures of Beau with his sister, Alli. Alli traveling with the team, Alli accompanying Beau to a movie premiere. Alli, her face painted, at a Wind playoff game. There were fewer pictures of her as she got older, though there was one disturbing website she found that featured younger siblings of famous people and countdowns to "being legal." She couldn't find any social media accounts for Alli, and Beau's had been run by his sports management company and hadn't been updated in forever.

She'd pored over articles about his retirement announcement. Announced in the middle of the last season and effective immediately, it had been a surprise to the hockey community. He'd given a press conference where he'd read a prepared statement, and as Beau had talked about his team-mates being family, he'd choked up. The expression on his face had been the same one she'd seen when he sat with her grieving family at their Thanksgiving table.

But her digging failed to uncover one important thing. Bristol couldn't find any connection between Beau the Wind hockey player with Beau the Hope Falls stranger.

In a fit of embarrassment and rage, she'd ripped the sheets off her bed intending to burn them. But they'd stayed in a ball at the bottom of her closet, and she was ashamed to admit that she'd buried her face in them more than once to catch his lingering scent on them.

How could she have been so wrong about him? As a mother, she was supposed to have first-rate instincts about impending danger. How had he made it past her? How had he convinced her that he was a good, kind man?

If she were completely honest, nothing in her digging had made him seem like anything but that. The only anomaly was his disappearance.

It looked as though once again she was left with questions and a hole in her heart. But this time she was anything but numb.

16

The day of Savannah and Vince's wedding dawned crisp and bright. Another overnight snow had blanketed Hope Falls in a fresh layer of white that Bristol pretended to admire when she dropped Violet off with Nolan.

She put on a happy face for her daughter, and she'd put one on for Savannah's big day, but alone in the car, driving past the over-the-top town Christmas decorations, she let herself sink into the miserable stew of hurt and sad and anger.

Bristol eased to a stop at the corner of Bluebird and Main and stared at the twelve-foot inflatable angel outside the Twin Cinemas.

A feeling of desperation overtook her. "Hope," she said staring at the smiling angel, "I need your help snapping out of this for Vanna today. Just some temporary angel magic, please?"

The angel's beige face remained blankly positive, and Bristol pulled away cursing herself and inflatable angels everywhere.

She pulled into the parking lot of the Hope Falls Community Church right behind Savannah, their mother, and two women weighted down with tackle boxes full of hair and makeup necessities. Bristol pasted a smile on her face, climbed out of her car, and grabbed the garment bag from the backseat.

"Hey bride!" she said cheerily.

Savannah looked back at her with red eyes and a sad smile. Mary had a similar expression. She could see both joy and sadness there. One daughter was getting married and starting a new life while another's had ended.

"What's wrong?" Bristol demanded. "Did Vince call it off to start preparing for tax season?"

Savannah, the ball-busting attorney, gave a sad little sniffle. "I'm so happy and sad at the same time I think I'm losing my damn mind."

Mary was gesturing wildly behind Savannah's back in a pantomime Bristol took to mean "fix your sister, now!"

"Let's focus on the happy," Bristol said, decisively. "When we look back at this day, we want to remember all the happy, right?"

Savannah sniffled. "I guess."

"That's the spirit. Now, this is really important. Does your beauty team have a hair dryer?"

"They have everything. But I already washed my h—"

She didn't get to finish the subject because Bristol hit her in the face with a snowball.

"Are you kidding me right now?" she shrieked. "It's my wedding day!"

Savannah Quinn never backed down from a challenge. She retaliated with her own snowy weaponry, and Mary looked on as her daughters chased each other around the church's parking lot chucking snow at each other.

A side door opened, and Pastor Harrison poked his head out. He was a young, bookish man who often wore jeans under his robes. "Everything okay out here?" A snowball smacked into the white washed stone a foot from his face.

"Girls!" Mary yelled. "Sorry, pastor. They're just working out some wedding day jitters."

"Well, uh, don't get cold feet on me," he joked before slipping back inside. Mary and the beauty team followed him, leaving the girls to their ridiculousness.

The battle for snow supremacy raged until Savannah caught Bristol by the hood of her jacket and flung her into a snowdrift. Bristol shrieked as Savannah straddled her chest and shoved a handful of snow in her face.

"There! Now who needs the hairdryer?" Savannah laughed.

"Do not laugh too hard! You'll pee on me!" Bristol yelped.

Savannah fell over, and they both lay on their backs under the snow coated oak tree admiring the snatches of blue sky that peeked through bare branches.

"God, that felt good," Bristol admitted.

"Hell, yeah. You know if Hope were here, we would have ganged up on her and probably shoved her head first into this drift," Savannah said dreamily.

"Totally," Bristol snickered. "She was such an easy target."

A tidal wave of snow launched itself out of the tree, landing on them with a spectacular "whump." They shrieked and sputtered, brushing their faces clean.

"What the hell was that?" Savannah demanded.

Bristol looked heavenward. "I think that was Hope."

~

HOPE HAD SHOWN up for her today. Of that Bristol was sure. And for the first time in weeks, she felt a spark of hopefulness burn to life inside her. It was going to be a good day, she decided.

She changed out of her snow-soaked clothes and slipped into the fleecy green maid of honor robe Savannah had given her. Her sister, in a matching robe, was getting her hair and makeup done while Tessa snapped away with her camera, capturing every step of the process.

Mary, a stickler for details, headed out for fortifying snacks and to check up on the rest of the family and wedding party.

"B, can you do me a favor?" Savannah asked without moving her lips that were being painted a festive pink.

"Sure, what do you need?"

"Can you poke your head into the sanctuary and make sure the trees are plugged in? I don't want anyone crawling around on the floor while people are being seated."

"On it," Bristol said, cinching the tie on her robe and slipping her feet into her slippers. "I'll be back in a minute."

She ducked into the hallway and walked straight into a wall. A male wall. A *familiar* male wall.

This wasn't happening.

"Oh, no. No. You are definitely not here right now."

Beau was dressed in a sleek, fitted navy suit and tie. His hair was combed, his beard neatly trimmed, and his warm hands were on her shoulders. He was here.

"Bristol—"

"No. No way! You can't be here. This is not okay!"

"You look beautiful." He said the words in a rush as if they had clawed their way out of him.

"And you look like a liar." A hot one. A big, gorgeous, sexy, steaming liar.

He steered her across the hallway away from the door.

"Let me explain."

"What are you doing here?" she hissed. "You can't be here. It's my sister's wedding day. And stop touching me!"

He held up his hands in a sign of peace. "Bristol, I know you're mad, but I can explain."

"No, you can't. I need to get my sister ready to walk down the aisle, not hash things out with a one-night stand."

"We weren't a one-night stand," he argued. "Don't make what we have something sad and—"

"And what?" she demanded. "Pathetic? You slept with me, and then you packed your bag and left town. Without a backwards glance, I might add."

"Bristol, listen to me," he gripped her arms with warm, callused palms. "I lied to you."

"No shit."

He squeezed harder. "I'm not a yoga instructor."

"Yeah, how's that hockey career going?" she said, jutting out her chin. "Evanko, right?"

He took a deep breath. "Look, I can't fix what I did between the two of us right this second. I will. I swear to you I will. But there's something even more important that I have to do right now."

She choked out a laugh. "Oh really? And what's that?"

"I want you to meet my sister."

Bristol shook her head. "What are you talking about?"

Beau let go of one of her arms and reached into his jacket pocket. "I'm talking about this." He pulled out a piece of paper and handed it over to her.

She snatched it out of his hand and opened it with a huff of impatience.

Bristol didn't notice that her knees had buckled or that

Beau had guided her over to a red velvet bench under a picture of the last supper. She didn't notice that he'd crouched down in front of her. All that registered for her was her hand-writing on the paper. Her handwriting inviting Hope's heart recipient to her sister's wedding.

17

"Your sister?" Bristol whispered, her voice thick with emotion.

Beau nodded. "My sister has Hope's heart."

Bristol swallowed hard through the emotion that choked her. So many feelings were careening through her system she wasn't sure if she could stand it. She met his gaze. She let her breath out on a shaky exhalation. "She's okay? I mean, the transplant..."

"She's great. Hope saved her life. You saved her."

Bristol choked on a sob, and Beau tried to pull her into his arms. But she shook her head and pushed him away. "Don't even think for a second that we're okay, Beau," she warned.

Undeterred, he sat down next to her crowding her on the narrow bench. He draped an arm around her shoulders and pulled her into his side. "I know I owe you a big explanation and a bigger apology, but I had to make sure that you and your family were... okay before I brought Alli here to meet you."

"Alli is really here? You brought her today?" Bristol asked.

Beau nodded. "Yeah. She's eighteen. She had a congenital

heart defect, and I thought..." he took a moment to compose himself. "I thought I was going to lose her last winter."

Bristol bit her lip hard, remembering how it felt outside the ICU knowing that a loss was coming.

"You and your family saved Alli's life. She wanted to come find you from the get go. The second thing she said when she woke up from transplant surgery was 'I need to say thank you.'"

"What was the first thing?"

"'Holy shit, I'm not dead.'"

Bristol choked out a sob and a laugh and this time didn't fight it when Beau pulled her into his lap. He tucked her head under his chin.

"Baby. I'm sorry. I'm so sorry. For Hope, for me leaving, for not letting Alli contact you right away... This entire year has been an emotional roller coaster. I came here just to make sure you and your family couldn't hurt her in any way. We've dealt with people before trying to get things from us because of me..." he trailed off lamely.

"Why did you sleep with me, Beau?"

"Because you're the most incredible woman I've ever met in my entire life."

"Then why did you leave?"

"Because I had to go talk to Alli before I made the decision to uproot her and everything she's ever known and move us to Hope Falls."

She shook her head. "Don't say that, Beau."

"I love you, Bristol. And not just because of a decision that you and your family made that saved my sister's life. I feel like I've loved you from the minute I was born. I've been waiting this whole time just to find you, and I'm not going to give up on us."

"You can't say that! You can't just come back here and say all the right things. I trusted you! Violet trusted you."

"I know, gorgeous. And I'm so sorry. But I had to talk to Alli before I promised you anything. She was my whole world. When she got sick... when we found out that the only thing that would save her was a transplant, I was wrecked. She's lived with me since I was twenty."

He ran his free hand through his hair. "I came here to make sure you and your family weren't the kind of people who would try to take advantage of her or me. And I fell for you. Hard. But I couldn't make promises to you until I'd talked to her."

"It isn't all or nothing, Beau! You could have told me. You could have not slept with me. You could have done a hundred things somewhere in between."

"I fucked up. A lot. I know it," Beau said. "But I'm here now, and I'm going to make this right for all of you. Especially you and Violet."

Bristol nodded and swallowed hard. "I get that you wanted to protect your sister. I wish I could have had that opportunity with my own," she said. "But then that would mean that your sister wouldn't be here. God, this is so fucked up."

She threw a surreptitious glance at the painting above her and murmured a silent apology.

"I know, baby. I know," Beau said, rubbing her arm.

"Is everything all right? Can I be of some assistance?" Pastor Harrison, already dressed in his collar and robe, poked his head out of his office. He looked over the reading glasses perched on his nose and frowned.

Aware of the picture they were making in the hallway of the church, Bristol felt like she should at least climb off of Beau's lap, but he wasn't having it. "We're fine here, Pastor

Harrison," she said weakly. He didn't look convinced but stepped back into his office.

She should pull away, stand up, and slap Beau at least. But Bristol felt frozen in place as she processed.

"She's here now?"

Beau nodded. "I'd like you to meet her if you're okay with that. Then you can introduce her to the rest of your family."

Bristol swiped a hand under her eyes. "This is a lot to take in. I thought maybe no one read my letter."

"I read it a thousand times. I had to come."

"I get it. You wanted to protect your family," she said, pulling a tissue out of the pocket of her robe.

But he was shaking his head. "It was more than that. That letter... it was like falling for a stranger. And that's exactly what I was doing. I was already halfway in love with you before I ever laid eyes on you."

He took the tissue from her and dabbed under her eyes. "At first I was terrified at the thought of introducing my sister to you, and now all I want is for you two to get to know each other. I've told her about you and—"

"Just stop, Beau," Bristol said, slicing her hand through the air. "I can't deal with all of this."

"Okay. Okay. One thing at a time," he slid her back onto the bench and rose. She missed the warmth as soon as it was gone and hated herself for it. "I'm going to go get her. You'll be here?"

Those green eyes were searching her face.

"I'll be here," she affirmed. *Because I'm a masochistic crazy person.*

He hurried off down the hall, and Bristol looked up at the painting again. "Well, I'm not asking you what you would do," she muttered.

She probably looked like a giant, weepy mess. And she was

still wearing a bathrobe, a detail that had escaped her when she'd gone into rage mode with Beau. Thank God she hadn't done her makeup yet.

He loved her? What in the hell could that possibly mean? People who loved each other didn't lie and disappear. They communicated. Or, at least, that's what she heard they did. Her only long-term monogamous relationship had been with her college sweetheart and didn't last long enough for their daughter to go to preschool.

Her inner tirade was cut off when Beau returned. He held the hand of a reed slim girl several inches shorter than Bristol. Her hair had the same reddish brown tones as Beau's beard, and she had a dusting of freckles over the bridge of her nose and cheeks. She had his green eyes, too, and they were filled with tears.

"Bristol, this is my—"

The girl didn't wait for her brother to finish the introduction. She launched herself into Bristol's arms. "Thank you," she whispered against Bristol's shoulder. "I don't know how to say it big enough or loud enough, but thank you."

Bristol's arms closed around the girl.

"It's nice to meet you," Bristol said, fighting off the wave of emotion that threatened to swamp her.

They stood, holding each other as Beau looked on.

"I have so many questions about Hope," Alli said, pulling back, her cheeks wet with tears.

"I have a lot of questions about you," Bristol said, giving the girl a watery smile.

"Hey, maid of honor, are you ever getting your ass back in here—What the hell are *you* doing here?" Savannah in a satin robe and flawless make-up demanded when she spotted Beau in the hallway. "What's going on?"

Pastor Harrison's door cracked open again. "Everything all right?" he asked the bride.

"I'm not sure, pastor," Savannah said. "But I'll let you know if I need a couple of acolytes to escort this gentleman out of here."

"That won't be necessary," Bristol said. "Vanna, this is Alli." Bristol took Alli's hand and led her over to Savannah.

"Nice to meet you, Alli, but I already have the final head-count to the caterer, so you can only eat appetizers at the reception," Savannah said dryly.

"I asked Alli to be here today," Bristol began. "She's Beau's sister."

"Swell. I hope you're better mannered than your idiot brother," Savannah said, turning back toward the room.

Alli's eyes widened as she shot a look at her brother.

Bristol stopped Savannah with a hand on her sister's arm. "She's also Hope's heart recipient."

A lesser woman would have collapsed, but not Savannah Quinn. Her sister shoved a finger in Bristol's face. "If you ruin my make-up, and I have to sit still for another hour I'm going to kill you. Sorry, Pastor Harrison," she said, throwing the apology over her shoulder.

Her attention returned to Alli, and Bristol saw Savannah swallow hard. "You have Hope's heart?" she asked, her voice trembling slightly.

Alli nodded and tapped her chest.

"I think I need a drink," Savannah said, sinking down onto the bench that Bristol and Beau had vacated. Pastor Harrison ducked back into his office and returned carrying a bottle of scotch and a stack of paper cups.

Bristol gave him a watery smile when he handed her a cup.

"So you knew this whole time," Savannah asked Beau. "You came to town knowing that we'd lost our sister?"

He nodded, and Bristol was relieved when he didn't try to explain himself.

"We'll deal with that later," Savannah said in a tone that let them all know she was far from overlooking Beau's omission. "But for now, Alli, I'm so honored that you came so that my other sister could be here on my wedding day." Her voice cracked, and Pastor Harrison pressed a cup into her hand and poured.

Bristol grabbed the box of tissues off the console below a stained glass window that was bathing the carpet in reds and golds. But Savannah shook her head. "No, I'm good. I'm not wrecking this perfection," she said. "How tall are you, Alli?"

"Five-foot-four," she said.

"She looks about the right size," Savannah said to Bristol.

Bristol slid an arm around her sister's waist. "Yeah, she does."

"Alli, how would you feel about being a bridesmaid?" Savannah asked.

"Are you sure? I know we've known each other for a very long thirty seconds, but I don't want you to make any rash decisions on your big day."

"I've got hair and make-up ready and waiting and a hunter green dress that will look amazing with your coloring. In or out?" Savannah said in her no-nonsense tone. "Keep in mind that saying no will ruin my entire day."

"Well, in that case, count me in," Alli decided.

Savannah nodded briskly and then rolled her eyes. "Oh, what the hell?" She pulled Alli in for a hug, and Bristol hastily dug a tissue out of the box. "Get in here, Bristol," Savannah demanded.

Bristol let them drag her into the embrace, and she saw Beau over Alli's shoulder, eyes misty, accept a cup from Pastor Harrison.

"Girls, Vince just arrived—," Mary's announcement to her daughters was cut off when she took in the scene. "What's going on?" She stood in her red floor length gown, her dark hair pulled back in an artful twist, leaving her face unframed. She looked ready for battle if that's what was necessary to give her daughter a perfect day. But no one could prepare for this news.

"Mom, this is Alli, Beau's sister," Bristol began. "She... they..." She wasn't sure how to say it without inciting a flood of emotions.

"Oh for God's sake," Savannah said. "Sorry, pastor. Mom, Alli has Hope's heart. She's here so Hope could be here with all of us today."

Mary's face crumpled like a sheet of tissue paper as the news sunk in. "My Hope?"

Bristol grabbed a fistful of tissues for her mother and arrived at her side as Pastor Harrison poured another scotch.

Mary looked from scotch to tissues and back again before knocking back the scotch first. Tears were already flowing down her cheeks.

"Mom! Stop crying this instant," Savannah demanded.

"I'm sorry, sweetie," Mary wailed. "This is the most generous gift."

Alli started crying and walked into Mary's arms. Savannah held up her empty cup to Pastor Harrison who, happy to help, refilled it.

Somewhere in the middle of her mother hugging both Alli and Beau and sobbing about how happy she was, the hallway got more crowded.

"What's wrong? What happened?" Bob, looking dapper in his rented tuxedo, rushed to his wife's side with Vince, Nolan, and Violet hot on his heels.

"Shit! I'm not supposed to see you!" Vince yelped at Savannah and clapped a hand over his eyes.

"Babe, it's so far beyond that at this point," Savannah told him.

"Beau!" Violet in her pretty purple dress shouted and threw herself into his arms. Beau picked her up and squeezed her tight.

"Hey, short stack. I missed you!"

Bristol felt dizzy with the energy of the moment... and the scotch.

The explanation was given again and Bristol felt her heart squeeze in her chest when Big Bob Quinn looked down at Alli, tears in his dark eyes, and asked her how her recovery was going. The tissue box was empty as was the bottle of scotch, and they'd managed to put a hurting on the vodka Pastor Harrison had magically produced before Savannah took control of the situation again.

"You two," she said pointing at Alli and Bristol. "Get inside for hair and makeup. Mom, can you track down a sewing kit? Alli's going to be a bridesmaid, and I want to make sure Hope's dress fits her."

Mary started to sniffle again but nodded.

"Dad, can you please spread the word to the rest of the family so we don't have a sob fest during the ceremony?"

"Anything my girl wants," he said, wiping his eyes with a handkerchief.

"Vince, I'll see your handsome face in thirty minutes."

Vince leaned in and planted an NC-17 kiss on his soon-to-be wife and Beau covered Violet's eyes as she groaned at the grossness.

They began to disperse, each tasked with a job. Bristol took Violet from Beau and led Alli into what Savannah had affectionately dubbed the war room. But her sister stayed behind in the hallway. "I need a word with you, Beau."

BEAU WATCHED his sister and the woman he loved disappear behind a closed door before turning to face Savannah. Even without her dress, she still looked like a bride or, perhaps, considering her displeased expression, a queen.

"You look beautiful," Beau began.

But she was shaking her head and crossing her arms. "Save it, Romeo. Do you love my sister?"

He nodded. "Yeah, I do."

"Then you've got a lot of making up to do, and she's not going to make it easy for you."

"Understood." He deserved that. He'd made mistake after mistake, but he was here to change the pattern.

"As Bristol's sister, I am one-hundred percent on her side. However, if you're here to make her happy, to treat her well, and to be part of our family, I'll support you."

"That means a lot to me, Savannah."

"Just don't fuck up like this again. Not cool, Beau."

"I'm going to make it up to her. I promise."

"You can start at the reception."

"On it," he nodded.

He watched her disappear into the room and slid down on the bench, his long legs stretching out into the now empty hallway. Bristol hadn't slapped him or tried to knock his teeth out. That was a good sign. He'd hurt her deeply, and it wasn't going to be easy to repair that wound. But he was willing to do whatever it took. She was his family now, even if she didn't realize it yet.

18

By the time Savannah marched down the aisle to her groom, the entire church and most of Hope Falls knew about Alli and Hope's heart. Weddings were usually emotional occasions, but when Savannah got to the end of the aisle, she'd pulled her parents, Bristol, Vince, and Alli into a group hug. There wasn't a dry eye in the entire church as every single person in the sanctuary rose to applaud.

Bristol hoped that Pastor Harrison was wearing a mic because otherwise the audio for the wedding video would be nothing but sniffles and nose blowing from the crowd.

The ceremony was blissfully short-lived and went off flawlessly. She felt the weight of Beau's gaze on her, never wavering. But she avoided looking at him except for the occasional glance every thirty or so seconds. Her parents had coaxed him into the front row with them and Violet where he sat and watched her like a hunter patiently waiting for his prey.

When Vince bent the laughing Savannah over backwards to lay a first kiss on her, the crowd cheered. Bristol glanced over her shoulder at Alli who was grinning wide, and in that moment, she felt Hope's presence in a soaring lift of spirit.

~

BY THE TIME the wedding party finished up with pictures, the reception was well underway thanks to a generous open bar.

Amanda and Justin Barnes had pulled out all the stops to turn Mountain Ridge's ballroom into a winter wonderland. A twelve-foot tree decked in lights stood guard over the ever-growing pile of wedding gifts beneath it. The rafters of the ballroom were strung with hundreds of white lights, and each table had an ivory tablecloth with its very own Christmas tree centerpiece. Accents of silver and gold clung to anything that would stand still. On the wall beyond the dance floor sat long tables laden with appetizers and swagged in gold tulle. The wall of glass that opened onto the large stone patio provided the perfect view of the light snow that had just begun to fall.

It was the perfect night to cap the perfect day for her sister. Savannah and Vince danced and laughed and accepted the well wishes of most of Hope Falls.

Bristol did her best to avoid Beau, but fate—and her dear sister—conspired against her. Somehow Savannah had managed to add Beau and Alli to the family table. Beau claimed the seat next to her while Alli sat between him and Mary who was beside herself with joy.

Lissa snuck up behind Bristol. "If he pulls anything, you tell me, and I'll threaten him with my butter knife," she whispered in Bristol's ear.

"I'll let you know."

An entree magically appeared in front of her, replacing the salad she hadn't touched, but she didn't do more than rearrange it on her plate. Her mind and heart were so full. Her body was painfully aware of Beau's presence, the nudge of his knee under the table, the texture of his suit jacket against her bare arm when he reached for the butter. She could feel the heat pump off his body and hated that she wanted to lean into that heat.

While her body paid exclusive attention to Beau's physical presence, she watched Alli intently, looking for signs of Hope. She was a pretty girl with her short crop of reddish hair. She sported a teeny stud that winked in her nose under the reception lights. Bristol wondered how protective big brother Beau felt about that. Alli chattered happily with Bristol's parents with a barely restrained energy that was refreshing. The girl had a new lease on life, and Bristol felt like she wasn't going to waste it. Hope would approve.

Just about every single reception attendee stopped by their table to introduce themselves to Alli and welcome her to Hope Falls. In Bristol's opinion, they were entirely too friendly toward Beau. Beau was still the enemy and should be treated as such. She excused herself abruptly from the table and got up.

Bristol ducked behind the massive tree and was heading for the side door, intent to grab a few seconds of alone time. But when the tingle raced up her spine, she knew she'd just allowed herself to be cornered by Beau.

"Bristol," he said, his large palms sliding down her bare arms.

The DJ announced a slow song for "all the Christmas lovers out there."

"Dance with me," Beau said, his voice low and heated when Dean Martin launched into *Let it Snow*.

"Give me one good reason why I should."

"So I can apologize again... and explain."

She should know better, Bristol thought as she let him pull her into his arms. Her whole body was on high alert as he wrapped her arms around his neck and settled his hands at her waist. When she tried to step back, create some space to breathe, Beau tightened his hold and pulled her closer.

"So talk," she said, pretending that she wasn't melting in his arms, fighting off the memories of his body over her, under her, inside her. Her breath froze in her lungs when her core clenched reflexively.

"I was drafted by the Wind out of high school," Beau began. "And in some ways, they felt like the first family I ever had. For two years, I trained, and I traveled. I partied a lot. Hockey was my entire life. And then my parents announced they were leaving the country to dig wells in Africa. Alli was only nine when she came to live with me, and that changed everything."

"Must have cramped your style," Bristol said, thinking of all those pictures of Beau and all those women.

"I grew up fast. I stopped fooling around, stopped partying. I never brought a girl home with me. The ones I was photographed with? They were all my teammates' sisters or cousins. I never dated any of them. I didn't want Alli to grow up thinking that's what women were valued for. To be honest, having her around made the whole team grow up. They had been my family, and that made them hers too. She was everyone's little sister, and none of us wanted to set a bad example for her."

Bristol could just imagine little Alli growing up around beefy hockey players. It made her smile, a little.

"But I couldn't protect her from everything," Beau continued. "In school, when kids found out who she was, who I was, they'd ask her for things. Tickets, autographs, jerseys. And the same thing happened to me on occasion. There was a girl who worked for a sports management company. We dated off and on for a few months until I found out she was just trying to get me to sign with the agency. Others just wanted money or the attention you get when you're associated with a professional athlete."

They swayed slowly to the music that neither was listening to.

"When she got sick, I retired. I couldn't be there for her like I needed to be and be on the road for the season. I didn't want to put Alli through the public spectacle of the 'poor PHL player and his dying sister.' And as much as those guys had my back on the ice, it's hard to be family when I wasn't part of the team anymore. So it's been just the two of us since last year."

Bristol didn't want to admit that she could empathize with him. She felt more comfortable with mad.

"So you came out here and lied to my face to make sure I wasn't trying to scam you out of money," she summarized, hunting for the anger again.

"I came here to make sure your family was safe for Alli to meet. You gave us the greatest gift on earth, but that doesn't mean I'm going to rush into an introduction when I know nothing about your family. What if you'd wanted something from her or me? How could either of us say no with what you did for us?"

"I just wanted her here today, Beau! I wasn't looking for a payout or media attention."

"I know that," he said, swaying to the music. "Alli and I wouldn't be here if that were the case. You and the Quinns were exactly the kind of people I'd hoped you'd be. Alli's missed out on that. A brother who was on the road half the year, parents who had no interest in her life. I wanted to give her normal."

"You did the best you could," Bristol said grudgingly.

"When she got sick, I thought it would be the catalyst that would bring our parents home. That now they wouldn't be able to ignore her." He shook his head sadly. "They never came home. They just told me to handle it and keep them apprised. There were funds to raise and forests to save and humanitarian missions to plan. They couldn't be bothered to put that aside and come home for their daughter even when she was on her death bed."

"I'm sorry, Beau. That's not what family should be like."

"I know what it should be like. After I spent time with you and Violet, when I had Thanksgiving with the rest of your family, that's when I knew what I wanted. I want a loud, sloppy, supportive, crazy family for me and for Alli. I want her to have you and the rest of the Quinns. I know this is a lot to take in in one day, but Alli and I are moving here. I'm staying, and I'm going to get a second chance with you. I want us to be a family together. You, me, Violet, and Alli."

Bristol stumbled and stepped on his foot. "Are you insane?"

"I think so," he said with a soft laugh. "I haven't thought about anything but you since I saw you at the rink that first moment. I looked at you, and I thought 'That's what my future looks like.'"

"Jesus, Beau!"

"I don't expect you to forgive me right here and right now. I know you'll make me work for it, and I love that about you. But please, Bristol, promise me you'll give me the opportunity to make it up to you."

"You lied to me, you slept with me, and then you just abandoned me."

He shook his head. "After we spent that night together, after I saw your family and how much they were still hurting over Hope, I knew I had to go home and talk to Alli. It took no convincing on my part to get her out here, and she already told me at the church she's staying."

"How the hell do you expect me to trust you again?"

"You know me, Bristol. You know I'm a good guy. I made a mistake—a big one," he acknowledged before she could point it out. "I'm willing to do whatever it takes to make this right."

"I don't think you understand. You lied to me, you lied to my family, you lied to my entire town. I let you into my home *with my daughter*. I slept with you. I never would have done that had I known who you really were."

"Baby." She could hear the hurt in his tone.

"Thank you for bringing Alli here today, Beau. It means the world to my family, but I just don't think I can forgive you for the rest." Bristol tried to free herself from his arms.

"Look at you two so cozy under the mistletoe," Sue Ann announced, appearing next to them in a red and green plaid skirt and sweater combination and looking pleased as punch.

Beau and Bristol looked up to see the berries and glossy green leaves hanging above their heads.

"You were such a rascal, Beau, fibbing like that. You're lucky your heart was in the right place, or you'd have a lot of explaining to do!" Sue Ann poked him in the chest. "Well, don't let me stop you. Mistletoe is serious business!"

Bristol thought about running for her life, but Beau would just catch her. And she didn't want to cause a scene at Savannah's wedding. She'd never live it down. A crowd was already gathering, all smiling expectantly. *Oh, how quick Hope Falls was to forgive.*

"Oh, hell. Just get it over with already," she muttered to Beau. But he wouldn't be rushed. He took his time, framing her face in his hands and lowering those firm lips to hers, taking what she didn't want to offer. It was a chaste kiss, but that didn't stop her body from erupting like a volcano. He didn't have to pull her closer, her body happily threw itself at him. The feel of him against her, the connection their bodies shared, was a painful reminder of what could have existed between them.

When he finally pulled back, people were cheering, and Bristol had to uncurl her fingers from the lapels of his jacket.

The song changed from Sweet Christmas Carol to Icona Pop, and before Bristol's eyes had refocused, Savannah was there, dragging her out on the dance floor. She looked over her shoulder at a disheveled and regretful Beau as she was led away.

19

The entire town of Hope Falls had gone stupid. Bristol thought she'd be able to count on resident outrage that Beau had lied to her face, swept her off her feet, and then vanished on her. He was an outsider who had misled an entire town.

However, Bristol had seriously underestimated Beau's charm.

Two days after Savannah's wedding, she and Violet had run into Mr. Maybry and Lauren Stevens, real estate agent and TV host extraordinaire, on the street outside Early Bird.

"Have you heard about your new neighbor?" Mr. Maybry, his white hair tucked under his ever-present baseball hat asked gleefully.

"I haven't," Bristol said. "Is the hardware store reopening?"

"Reopening with myself at the helm, and the second and third floors are going to be renovated into apartments," Mr. Maybry announced proudly, his white moustache obscuring part of his smile.

"That's wonderful!" Bristol said, pressing a kiss to his cheek. "I'm so happy to have you back."

Violet beckoned him down to her level. "Will there be lollipops?"

He chuckled and rummaged through his jacket pockets before producing a lollipop. "For you, my dear, there will always be lollipops."

"This is so great!" Violet said, shredding the wrapper and popping the candy into her mouth.

"So who's the proud new owner?" Bristol asked.

Lauren suddenly became very distracted by her phone, and Bristol felt the pit of her stomach drop out.

"That's the best part!" Mr. Maybry clapped his hands. "This big time hockey player and his sister are moving here and—"

"Beau Evanko bought the building?" Bristol asked Lauren accusingly.

"Oh, hey! Look at the time. Mr. Maybry and I have to meet the contractors, so we'll just get out of your way." Lauren hustled him through the door of the hardware store before Bristol could ask any more questions.

"Mom, is Beau going to be our neighbor?" Violet asked.

She hoped not. She really, really hoped not.

The next morning, she was helping Edwin get ready to open Early Bird when she spotted Beau heading for the front door of Lucky's gym. She was going to put an end to this idiocy once and for all.

She stormed out of the restaurant and crossed the street. "Hey, Beau!"

He turned at his name, and his face lit up when he saw her barreling at him.

"No! Do not make that face. This is not a happy visit," she snapped.

"I can't help how I look at you," Beau said, grinning at her irrational demand.

"You're not moving to Hope Falls, you're not buying the hardware store building, you're not weaseling your way back into my life." She jabbed a finger into his chest with every item on his "not doing" list.

"Gorgeous, you know I hate to disagree with you. But I already moved to Hope Falls, and I already bought the hardware store and building. And I will earn a second chance with you. I'm willing to wait as long as it takes. I will wear you down."

"You are insane."

"I'm not insane. I'm hopeful," he corrected.

"Why are you trying to ruin my life?" Bristol demanded and barely resisted stomping her foot.

His face turned serious, and he cupped his hand to her cheek. "Bristol, I'm not doing any of this to hurt you. I love you. Now put this on and go back inside."

He shucked off his jacket, which was eight sizes too big for her and tucked her into it. He gave her a quick kiss on the cheek and then pushed her in the general direction of Early Bird.

She'd stormed out of her place of business without a coat in the dead of winter to scream at a man in the street. In a normal town, no one would ever find out about her mini breakdown at five in the morning. But not Hope Falls.

No, she spent the entire morning listening to people advise her on how to forgive him and say things like "what a lovely man that Beau Evanko is." While the subtle ones sang his praises, the bold ones laid it all out for Bristol.

"Mark my words. You wait too long to forgive this one, and someone else will be less stupid and more forgiving and snatch him away," warned Renata Blackstone, pointing an unpainted finger at her.

"Look, honey. We want you to be happy, and the rest of us

can see clear as day that that boy loves you. You've got to give him a second chance. You're meant to be," Sue Ann had announced at the head of the line.

The seven people behind her waiting to order all nodded in agreement.

"You really have to think about this, Bristol. Hope brought him here. It's fate," Marlene Brooks from Two Scoops called out.

Life couldn't be this against her, Bristol insisted.

But it was, and it continued to be. He ate at Early Bird every damn morning. Margo and Edwin ignored her orders to stop serving him and fed him whatever his cruel, lying heart desired. And she caught herself looking at him every five seconds or so because who wouldn't? He seemed to get better and better looking just to torture her. And, of course, he was the one to grab the mop when she failed to secure the lid on the fresh thermos of dark roast and proceeded to dump it all over the floor. And, of course, he hopped behind the counter and grabbed an apron and ran dishes from kitchen to counter when Maya called in sick.

When Bristol filled in for a shift at Sue Ann's, Beau and Alli showed up for dinner. When she showed up at her parents' house for Sunday lunch, Beau and Alli were there. She'd tried to sneak out the back door while Beau shoveled the walkway out front, but Alli had barred her way and insisted she stay and chat.

Construction started immediately next door, and the *Hope Falls Gazette* gleefully printed a front page interview with Beau about his plans for Pollard's Hardware and the building. Rumor had it he was also working on some top secret deal with Lucky Dorsey.

Beau showed up for Violet's next hockey game but stayed in the stands where, instead of being picked apart by angry parents, he signed autographs and cheered next to Nolan. Lissa, for her part, wasn't as big of a sucker for Beau as the rest of town and stationed herself behind the team bench to give Bristol her support. When Violet scored a goal, Bristol happened to peer over her shoulder and catch Nolan and Beau jumping to their feet and chest bumping.

That's when she realized she was going to have to resign herself to Beau's presence in Hope Falls.

"WHAT?" Bristol grumbled into the phone. She'd fallen asleep on the couch yet again in yet another prime example of the sad, single mother life when her daughter was spending the night with her father and stepmother. The incessant ringing of her phone broke through her sleep fog.

"Have you seen Alli?" Beau's voice was frantic on the other end.

Bristol sat up and yawned. "No, is she missing?"

"She was acting all mopey and angsty today, and when I came back from picking up snacks, she was gone. She left a note saying she caught a ride into town with Shelby."

"Did you try her phone?" Bristol asked, hurrying into her bedroom for pants and shoes.

"No, I didn't think of that. Of course I tried her phone, genius."

"Add that to the list of things Beau needs to apologize to Bristol for," she grumbled, shoving her feet into a pair of fleece-lined boots.

"Sorry. I'm sorry, Bristol. I'm just..."

"Worried. I know. It's going to be fine. It's Hope Falls. There's no bad side of the tracks here. You take this side of

Main Street, and I'll work on the other. I'll text you if I find her."

"Thank you. I love you. You're literally the best woman in the world."

"Don't make this weird. I'm not doing you a favor. I'm doing Alli a favor. Got it?"

"I still love you."

"Ugh!" She hung up on him and ignored the warm, gooey sensation in her chest. Bristol grabbed a hat and her parka and headed out the door.

She crossed the street and peeked into Lucky's gym, which was dark and empty. The fire station was buttoned up tight, too. Alli was probably just working out some teenage stuff that an overbearing older brother couldn't help with... or maybe even caused. It hadn't been that long since Bristol had been a teenager. She remembered what it was like to feel misunderstood and lost. Hell, she felt that way now.

A thought struck her as she crossed the street and headed toward the used bookstore. Hope, in all her goodness, had more than her fair share of angst as a teenager, and there was one spot that she habitually visited when she was feeling particularly angsty.

It was a long shot, but it was better than wandering around the deserted downtown in frigid winter temperatures.

Bristol turned off of Main Street and headed toward the green of Riverside Recreation Area. The park boasted tall, snow-laden pines and a meandering paved path that paralleled the river. A large picnic area was tucked away in the evergreens and served as the backdrop for the Annual Christmas Eve Carnival. It was a peaceful patch of nature right in Hope Falls' own backyard and it was decked out in Christmas light finery. The trees twinkled with lights. The lampposts that lit the path were decked with silvery snowflakes. And the evergreens that flanked the pavilion were drenched in cheerful colored lights.

Bristol wandered the familiar path and enjoyed the special silence that only a winter night could provide. Life had become noisier since Beau's return, since the entire town seemed hell bent on getting her to forgive him. There were moments, brief and bright, that had her wondering why she was carrying the grudge.

She had a gorgeous man capable of making her feel again, who insisted that he was in love with her and wanted to carve out a spot in her family, her life, her town. But still she hesitated. As attracted as she was to him, he had lied to her.

It came down to loyalty, she thought. Beau was loyal to Alli and the small family they'd built. Bristol understood that and could even respect it. She felt the same protectiveness toward her own family. But Beau had put his family above hers, and while she could understand the circumstances and the decision on his part to continue the deception, she just wasn't ready to forgive it.

She wanted to. The way Violet looked up to Beau, the way Alli fit so well with the Quinns, the way Beau looked at her—she wanted it all. But how could she move past the deception? She needed more time, and if she was honest with herself, she thought that, if Beau had more time, he would very likely change his mind. What could she offer him that any one of those beautiful women he'd dated couldn't? What could Hope Falls give him that Chicago and an exciting career couldn't? She didn't want to commit and get attached only for him to change his mind.

A splash from the river caught her attention and through the dim light from the lamppost behind her, she spotted a lone figure leaning morosely on the walking bridge over the water.

For a second her heart stopped. It was Hope's bridge. This was the spot that her sister would come to when she needed to work out something particularly teenager-y, tossing stones into the water just as the figure was doing now.

"Alli?"

"Oh, geez. Did Beau send you? He seriously needs to get a life. I'm eighteen, and I can't even take a walk by myself?"

Bristol stepped onto the bridge, still rocked to find Alli in the same spot Hope had spent so much time in.

"He was worried."

"I swear to God he thinks I'm going to drop dead of a heart attack if I'm not under 24/7 supervision," Alli said, tossing another rock into the black waters beneath the bridge.

"Uh, can you blame him? You almost died."

"Well, I'm alive now, aren't I?"

Clearly Alli wasn't thrilled with that reality at the moment.

"Wanna talk?" Bristol asked, sliding into the position she'd assumed when Hope needed talked down from something. She slid her legs between supports and let them dangle into space.

"No," Alli said definitively. "I don't have anything to say. It's not like I have anything worthwhile to say anyway. I'm not her!"

"Who?"

Alli rolled her eyes. "Hope. I'm not Hope."

"Who said you should be?" Bristol wasn't sure if pointing out the fact that Alli was currently acting exactly as eighteen-year-old Hope had would hurt or help.

"No one. Everyone." Alli threw her arms up toward the sky. "It's like everyone is telling me what an amazing person she was, and that's serious pressure, you know?"

"What do you mean?" Bristol was stymied now.

Alli flopped down next to her and dangled her legs over

the side of the bridge. "A trauma surgeon? I mean seriously, couldn't she have been a guidance counselor or a daycare provider? Something normal? Do you know what kind of pressure I'm under now? I have the heart of a girl who saved lives and not just by dying. EMT, medical school, residency," Alli ticked Hope's accomplishments off on her fingers. "How am I going to live up to that?"

Bristol grabbed her arm. "By living, dummy. You didn't take Hope's place. You didn't end her life. You got a great, amazing, wonderful gift, and now you need to go spend your life following *your* dreams. Not someone else's."

Alli took a deep shuddering breath. "I don't want to let you down," she said, tears glistening in her emerald eyes. "If it weren't for you, I wouldn't be here today."

"Ah, crap," Bristol threw her arms up and looked up at the night sky. "A little help here! We don't know what the hell we're doing down here, Hope!"

Alli sniffled wetly, and Bristol sighed. She dug out a tissue from her pocket stash that she kept religiously replenished and handed it over. "Look. I have no idea how to process this either from my end. Yes, my sister was an incredible person, a hero. But the girl I miss? She wasn't Wonder Woman. She snort laughed and couldn't drink soda without getting the hiccups. I miss *that*. And I think it sucks that she had to die, and I think it's amazing that you are here getting a second chance. It makes it seem like less of a waste, you know?"

"I guess so." Alli blew her nose. "It's like I'm so happy and so sad at the same time. I'm here, but your sister isn't. What's so important about me that I get to live when her life ended? And what if I fuck it all up?"

"Alli, I don't think you're here because she died. I think it was her time. Period. And we thankfully just made the right call afterwards. You're not going to fuck it all up," Bristol sighed.

"How do you know?"

"Well, for one, your brother won't let you."

"Beau is driving me insane. He's up my ass all the time, making sure I feel okay and that I'm taking my meds and blah blah blah."

"He thought he was going to lose you. He's entitled to be an overprotective ass for a little while. If the timing hadn't been exactly right, he could be missing you right now instead of smothering you."

"He's in love with you, you know."

Bristol rolled her eyes heavenward again. "He's got a funny way of showing it."

"Look, I probably don't need to tell you this, but Beau is incredibly protective. He once knocked a guy's teeth out on the ice for running his mouth about me when I was fifteen."

"That's disgusting."

"That's hockey," Alli smirked. "But my point is, he came here to make sure that there were no threats to me before telling me about your letter. He wanted to play the overprotective big brother card yet again. I'd been asking to meet you since the surgery, and I didn't even know about the letter. He told me he was spending Thanksgiving with friends on the West Coast."

"Oh, well at least I'm not the only woman he lies to."

Alli lifted a shoulder. "All I'm saying is I met your family, and I know there's nothing you wouldn't do to protect them. Beau came here thinking he was protecting me, and instead he got kicked in the balls with love. I think he was half in love with you before he even got here. When he finally showed me your letter, the folds were so deep I thought he must have read it a million times."

Bristol sighed. "I get that he was protecting you. But he continued to lie long after he assessed my threat level."

"Well, he's a guy. He was in over his head, and he realized that nothing but the biggest, most heartfelt, most over-the-top apology was going to fix this."

"Oh, really? And when am I going to witness that?"

Alli studiously avoided eye contact. "I guess we'll see."

They sat in silence for a few minutes surrounded by the twinkle of Christmas lights and the glitter of snow.

"I know I'm fighting it right now, but do you think there's a possibility this was all... I don't know... meant to be?" Alli asked.

"Like fate?" Bristol prompted.

"Think about it," Alli said. "Hope dies, you make the call on donating her organs, and boom—my life is saved. Beau comes out here and falls head over ass in love with you, drags me out here, and we all just... fit. Your family is awesome. You're exactly what my friends had growing up. Don't get me wrong, Beau was awesome to me. But we both missed out on this. I don't think any of this is a coincidence."

"You think Hope is out there pulling these ethereal puppet strings?" Bristol wasn't sure if she was appalled or comforted by the thought.

"I kinda do," Alli shrugged.

Had Hope sent her Beau and Alli? Was that even a possibility? And what would it mean if she rejected Beau and his demands for a second chance. *Would she be turning her back on her sister?*

"So what do you want to do with your life?" Bristol asked, desperate to change the subject.

Alli snorted, effortlessly shifting gears back into her downward spiral. "I have no clue! I'm eighteen, and I have to redo my senior year of high school. I really don't think I'd be a good trauma surgeon, though. I puke when I see blood unless it's on the ice."

"You don't have to be Hope," Bristol groaned. "You have to be happy. What makes you happy?"

"How the hell should I know?"

Bristol laughed. "What about puppies? Everybody loves puppies?"

Alli gave a mournful, one-shoulder shrug. "I guess they're okay."

"Okay, now you're just being insane," Bristol teased.

The corner of Alli's mouth turned up. "It's just a lot of pressure, you know? Second chance, Hope's heart—it's a really big deal, and I don't want to screw it up."

"Look at it this way. You get a second chance to really choose the life you want to have, not just whatever path you were on before. And my sister finally gets to have some fun living through you."

"Go on," Alli said with suspicion.

"My sister spent most of her last few years in classrooms and crashing in on-call rooms. She missed out on the normal fun rights of passage that the rest of us enjoy because she was so focused on her goals. For Savannah's bachelorette party, Hope actually suggested we hit happy hour at the bar down the street from her hospital."

Alli snorted.

"She had no clue what fun was, except for the Christmas Eve Carnival and her movie nights with Violet and me. You're her second chance at fun. Make out with boys, do a naked 5k, jump in the car and drive to the beach with friends for a weekend. Make the most of your time here. That's the best way to honor Hope's heart and your own second chance."

"Wow," Alli frowned. "You're really good at this."

"Awh. Thanks. I need the practice. My daughter will be you in ten years."

"Beau would have just been like 'You have a new heart! Stop fucking it up and be happy!'" she said in a deep baritone.

"That's a really reasonable impression of him," Bristol said, taking her phone out of her pocket. "Listen, I'm going to text him and tell him you're alive and well."

"Ugh, fine," Alli groaned. "But I don't want to go back so he can hover over me and hound me about when I think you're going to forgive him."

"How do you feel about frozen pizza rolls and peanut butter and jelly sandwiches?" Bristol offered.

"Do these foods involve me not going back to the B&B?"

"You can stay at my place tonight. I'm sure you and your brother could use some quality time apart."

"Yes please! As long as you promise not to tell me Hope also adopted eighteen children from third-world countries and won a Nobel Prize."

"Deal. As long as you don't try to convince me to give your brother a second chance."

20

*B*eau reluctantly agreed to not storm Bristol's loft and retrieve his sister, and with Alli in borrowed sweats and hair ties, they foraged for late night snacks. Bristol paused, pizza rolls in hand, when she witnessed Alli dumping a handful of potato chips on the peanut butter side of the open sandwich she was artfully crafting on the counter.

Some people received reassurances from the dead in the form of butterflies or birds or dreams. Hope sent hers in the form of snow to the face and a blatant disregard for sandwich traditions.

"You want chips in yours?" Alli asked, glancing up at Bristol.

"Yeah. Yeah, I do."

"There's no reason to get all weird about it." Alli frowned, and Bristol laughed.

She waited until Alli fell asleep on the couch under a blanket before tip-toeing back to her room and dialing Beau.

"Everything okay? She didn't run off on you too, did she?" He sounded worried and wide awake.

"Everything's fine," Bristol promised. "She's sound asleep on the couch. We talked and..."

"And did she tell you what the hell's wrong with her?"

Bristol laughed softly. "She was feeling some unintended pressure to live up to her new heart."

Beau swore.

"Don't worry. I told her no one here is telling her she needs to follow in Hope's footsteps. She just needs to live her own life to the fullest."

Beau sighed, and Bristol could picture him running a hand through his messy hair.

"Thank you for that, Bristol. Sometimes she doesn't want to hear things from her big brother."

"I think her exact words were 'big, overbearing brother'," Bristol teased.

"Yeah, well. She's no walk in the park either."

"Actually, she was. I literally found her when I was walking in the park. Same spot Hope used to go to work things out."

"What are the odds of that?" he asked.

"About as good as Alli putting chips in the PB&Js we made when we came back here."

There was a beat of silence. "She never did that before the surgery," Beau admitted. "And I didn't notice it at first, but then I got your letter, and it just made sense. I never mentioned it to her."

"I didn't say anything to her. I didn't think she needed another comparison between her and Hope. But... I guess I just wanted to tell you."

"Thank you, gorgeous."

She took a deep breath. "I've been thinking," Bristol began. "About you and me."

"And?" She heard it—the anticipation, the worry—in his tone.

"And your sister has my sister's heart, and maybe that's not a coincidence."

"Maybe not," he agreed softly.

"We're connected, obviously, and that connection isn't just going to go away."

"Sooo..." he drew the word out.

"So maybe I should consider the possibility of maybe giving you a second chance." She bit her lip and held her breath.

"You definitely should concretely jump wholeheartedly into giving me a second chance."

"I'm nowhere near the realm of talking about your crazy 'move to Hope Falls and get married and make babies' scenario," she warned him.

"We can talk about that next week," he interjected.

"But maybe we can sort of practice seeing each other."

"I think you're a very smart woman, Bristol Quinn. I'll see you for breakfast tomorrow. Unless..."

"Unless what?"

"Unless you want me to come over tonight."

Bristol hugged her knees into her chest. "I'm not prepared to have both Evankos over for a sleepover tonight. I'll see you at breakfast."

AN HOUR LATER, Bristol was lying on her back staring up at the ceiling thinking about Beau when her phone signaled a text. It was Beau.

Are you awake?

She bit her lip and, for once, didn't try to push away the spark of excitement.

Wide. You?

He responded immediately.

Can't sleep. I'm outside.

Bristol jumped out of bed and looked out her window. Sure enough, there was Beau in a gray SUV.

He saw her looking and waved sheepishly.

She pulled the curtain back and blew out a breath. Decision time. If she was serious about a second chance, it at least warranted a face-to-face conversation.

She pulled a sweatshirt over her tank top and quietly snuck out the door. The frigid night air froze her bare legs until she climbed into the passenger seat. He already had the seat warmer on for her.

"Where are your pants?" Beau demanded gruffly, staring at the rainbow print shorts she wore.

"Upstairs with my better judgment. What are you doing here in your pajama pants at one o'clock in the morning?"

"I had to make sure you were serious about this whole second chance. I don't want to give you the whole night to reconsider." He picked up her hand and laced his fingers through hers. "Are you sure?"

She took a deep breath. "I think so. I just, I kind of thought you'd change your mind. What is the possible draw of me and Hope Falls over everything you've built for yourself in Chicago?"

"I'm not sure how to explain this so it doesn't sound like I drank Hope Falls' Kool-Aid," he said with a laugh. "But I'm going to try. My whole life was hockey until Alli moved in with me. Then it was hockey and Alli. You don't go into a professional sport planning to play it for the rest of your life. You try to maximize your career in the time you have, and then you move on."

"Okay, that makes sense."

"But I hadn't even started thinking about what I'd do after.

It was on my radar, but it was something I could put off thinking about for another season or two. And then Alli got sick, really sick. It was the middle of last season, but I needed to be there for her. So I walked away. The guys all knew. We were like brothers, and I miss them every day. But it was the right decision."

"And then she got better," Bristol said.

"Alli got Hope's heart, and it was a long recovery, but yeah, she got better. And then I realized I had no idea what I wanted to do with my life. We'd been in crisis mode for so long that having the luxury of planning for the future was completely foreign to me. And that's when I got your letter."

He pulled her hand to his mouth and pressed a kiss to her knuckles. The bristles of his beard tickled her skin.

"That letter gave me something to think about besides the empty, scary future. It gave me something that I could do in that moment. I could come out here to vet you and your family, thank you in whatever way appropriate, and then I could get back to trying to figure out what the hell to do with my life. Alli's eighteen and healthy now. I wasn't going to be needed as her caretaker or her guardian anymore. And without her and hockey, I was directionless. Until I saw you."

Bristol took a deep breath. "Can I ask you what you would have done if you thought me or my family were after something from you?"

Beau leaned forward. "I would have given you anything that you wanted. Just not Alli."

She shook her head and groaned. "So you really are this great guy who did a stupid thing?"

"Pretty much."

She sighed and turned to face him. She looked into those earnest green eyes that were searching hers for something, an answer or maybe a question.

"Okay."

"Okay what?"

"Okay, let's do this."

His quick intake of breath told her he'd worried himself half to death that she had changed her mind. And it instantly made her feel more confident in her decision.

"Ground rules, though," she warned.

"Passing food if your arms aren't broken?"

She grinned. "That and you can't lie to me anymore. I want to be able to trust you. I need to be able to trust you. I need to trust you around Violet, too. No lying or disappearing once you're officially in her life. I don't know how she'll take the news of us dating, but I want to be honest with her."

His smile stopped her. "What? What do you know?"

"That day at Two Scoops after her hockey game?"

"Yeah?"

"She had a little sit-down with me and asked me to consider dating you."

"You're freaking kidding me! My daughter asked you to date me?"

He nodded. "She was worried about you. She wanted you to find someone to date or marry, and the little Einstein that she is decided you'd have more time to find a boyfriend slash husband if she spent more time with Nolan and Lissa."

Bristol's mouth fell open and she flopped back against the seat. "My *eight-year-old daughter* thought I needed a man in my life, and that's why she asked to start spending more time at Nolan's?"

He squeezed her hand. "It had nothing to do with her not wanting to spend time with you. In fact, she'd like you and I to take her to the movies when we start dating."

"I think I'm going to cry," Bristol whispered. "When she

gets back from her dad's tomorrow, I'm going to hug her until she suffocates."

"And then we can take her to the movies?"

"Yeah, probably," Bristol laughed.

He turned serious again. "I need to know that you're sure about this. And by that, I mean I'm asking you if you understand that I intend to stay here and marry you and build a family with you."

Bristol put her head between her knees. "I'm just getting used to the idea of dating you. Can we start there?"

"Of course, gorgeous, but you need to know where I'm headed. And we can take our time getting there, but that's what I'm in this for. I want you, me, Violet, and Alli to be a family."

"I appreciate and am terrified by your honesty."

"That's what you can expect from me from here on out. Barring surprises of course."

"Surprises?"

"You know, like Christmas presents."

"Of course, I get a boyfriend the week before Christmas, and now I have to shop for him," she grumbled.

"You are my present."

Bristol stared through the windshield that was rapidly fogging. "I can't believe this. This whole night can't be real. Can it? I'm going to wake up in the morning, and none of this will have happened, and I'll feel devastated... or maybe relieved."

"Devastated," he predicted. "Definitely devastated."

"I guess the only way to make sure is to seal the deal," she said, holding out her right hand.

He looked down at it and then back at her with a wolfish smile. "That's not how I seal deals with my future wife, gorgeous."

He grabbed her hand and pulled her across the console until she was straddling him. He shoved his fingers into her hair. "I love you, Bristol Quinn."

"I'm very fond of you, Beau Evanko."

He pulled her down to him, fusing his mouth to hers. Bristol felt the playfulness abandon them both as the kiss heated up. She'd missed this, missed him. His body was hard and strong beneath her. He was already raging hard, and Bristol shifted so she could feel the friction of his erection against her hungry center.

"God, Bristol, I missed you so damn much," he said, breaking the kiss.

She caught her breath and dove back in. His hot mouth teased her while he slipped his hands under her sweatshirt and the tank beneath that.

When his palms slid up to cup her bare breasts, he groaned into her mouth. "You're so built, baby. You fit me so perfectly." He let his thumbs stroke over her hardening nipples while she grinded against him. Two thin layers of clothing separated them, and that knowledge drove her insane.

"Please tell me you have a condom," she begged, kissing his neck.

"Oh, God. Wallet. There's one in my wallet," he gasped.

She found it in the cup holder and dug out the foil packet while Beau continued to worship her breasts with his hands. They felt full and heavy, and her tender peaks were begging for more.

"Beau," she shivered out his name. She was desperate for him. Her needy center wept for him to fill her. "I can't go slow, okay? Not this time." She wanted him fast and needy and desperate.

"Take everything you need." He yanked her shirts up and latched on to one breast as she levered herself up.

She didn't have to work hard to free him from his pants. His cock was already fighting its way over the waistband. Bristol used her teeth to rip open the packet, and Beau groaned. "You're a fucking fantasy come to life."

She held his shaft still with one hand and rolled on the condom with her other. The cords in his neck stood out as he fought to hold himself back.

"Open your eyes, Beau," Bristol breathed.

She waited until that molten green bore into her before sliding the crotch of her shorts to the side and taking him into her inch by inch. "Ah, fuck, yes," he gritted out. "Bristol, baby, you were made for me. I've been waiting my whole life for you."

She was so full and so impossibly wet for him. His hands came back to life on her breasts, and the second she felt those rough palms skim over her sensitive tips, she knew she was too far gone.

She levered up until she was almost empty and then slammed back down, tearing a cry of pleasure from her own throat.

"Baby, you have to go slower," Beau warned as she did it again.

But she shook her head. "No, now," she whispered. "Now, Beau."

They hung on for another thrust and then another, but when his lips parted over her nipple, when his tongue lashed over it, she felt herself let go.

"I feel it, Bristol. I feel you getting ready for me, baby."

He jerked his hips into her on her next slide down his shaft, and the angle, the perfect friction, set them both off. He grunted as he jerked inside her again and again while her channel milked his release with her own. She rode him hard, her breath coming in short, jerky pants until they were both too weak to move.

"You're it for me Bristol," he whispered, kissing her cheeks, her forehead, her hair. "I want this forever."

"Beau, I don't know what to say. I want to take things slowly, but when you say things like that, when you make me feel like this, it's hard to go slow."

"That's what I'm counting on, gorgeous," he said, cupping her face gently. "I want to sweep you off your feet. We've already gone too long without each other."

Flashing red and white lights glimmered through the fogged up windows and caught their attention. Still straddling him, Bristol swiped a hand over the window and looked on in horror as Deanna Dorsey and a team of firefighters gaped at them from the fire truck pulling out of the station.

Beau waved weakly while Bristol yanked her shirts down and buried her face in his neck. "Oh my God. Oh my God," she chanted.

"Safe to say we're probably never living this down, right?" Beau guessed.

21

The crowd at the Christmas Eve Carnival seemed significantly larger than usual, and Bristol wondered if Hope Falls had experienced a population boom she was unaware of. A pack of kids she'd never seen before raced past laughing. "Geez, we must have attracted half of Longview to the carnival," she guessed.

"This is just awesome," Alli said, hugging herself in the new purple parka Beau had given her. "I love this place!"

Bristol couldn't help but grin. In this moment, Alli reminded her so much of Hope that it hurt but in a good way. She loved catching these glimpses of the sister she'd lost in the sister she'd gained.

In somewhat of a Christmas miracle, she'd started to trust Beau again. The slate had been wiped clean. He hadn't come to Hope Falls to hurt her, and he'd done his best to prove that. He was a hard man not to love, not that she was ready to admit that to anyone but herself, of course. She'd known him a month, barely. She was an adult, a mother. She couldn't just jump into love and throw caution to the wind. She had to make sure everything fit in the right places.

Alli surprised her by throwing her arms around her. "Do you know what it feels like to have the first Christmas Eve of the rest of your life when you thought you'd already had your last?"

"What are you going to do with that life?" Bristol asked, fighting the tickle of tears in her throat.

"Well, for starters, I'm finishing high school in Hope Falls, and then I thought I'd start looking at West Coast colleges. But not medical schools."

Bristol laughed.

Alli led her through the crowd to the makeshift grandstand set up in front of the pavilion where the pie and Santa contests were in full swing. Mayor Henry Walker was there and had his head together with Sue Ann and Beau.

"What is your brother doing up there?" Bristol frowned.

Alli smiled innocently. "Oh, you know Beau, always making friends."

"You know something! What's going on?" Bristol demanded.

"Remember when I was talking about that over-the-top gesture from Beau?"

"Yeah," Bristol sighed.

"Well, it's happening,"Alli grinned. "Right now. Stay here, and do *not* move a muscle."

"What are you talking about?" But it was too late. Alli was already making her way onto the stage.

"Now you all just stand right here," Sue Ann announced, herding the rest of the Quinns over to Bristol. "We've got a little surprise worked out for you tonight."

Bristol's dad looked queasy. "The last time anyone in town surprised me, it was when Renata Blackstone paid for her oil change with a smudging ceremony. Damn garage still smells like that sage crap," he grumbled.

"What the hell is going on?" Savannah demanded, looking fierce despite her red and white pom-pom hat.

"Mom? What's the surprise?" Violet asked, clutching a cup of hot chocolate between her mittens.

"I don't know, sweetie. I'm sure it's very nice." *Please don't let it be something awful or embarrassing*, Bristol sent up the silent plea.

"Excuse me, ladies and gentlemen." Mayor Walker leaned into the mic, tapping it for attention. "I'd like to thank you all for coming out tonight to celebrate this magical time of year. It does this old man's heart good to see us come together time and again as a community, especially when it's for our own."

The applause was enthusiastic but muffled by gloves and mittens.

"We lost a special Hope Falls resident earlier this year. Hope Quinn was as good as you get, and her absence is felt every day by all of us. We've grieved with the Quinns, and we've watched them carry on as best they can as we felt help-less. So when Beau here came up with this idea, we were thrilled. Beau, why don't you say a few words?"

Bristol stared at him hard, trying to see inside him and understand what he was up to with the help of her traitorous town. He took front and center and leaned over the micro-phone. "Hi, everyone. I'm Beau, and this is my sister, Alli."

Alli waved cheerfully to the crowd.

"As most of you know, we got the most incredible gift from the Quinn family, and when you get a gift like that, a thank you card isn't going to cut it. And we aren't the only ones who want to say thank you. So if all of the Quinns will come up here, we've put a little something together for you."

He was looking at her, addressing the crowd but seeing only her. Reluctantly, she followed her family on stage where they formed a Quinn wall of support. But when she tried to position herself at the end of the line, Beau crossed to her, took her hand, and dragged her back to the mic with him. "Before we begin, I'd just like to say that not only do I owe this family a thank you, but I also owe this woman an apology."

The crowd of people she'd known since she was learning to walk tittered appreciatively. At least she wasn't the only sucker for a handsome face and sweet manners. He'd swept the whole damn town off its feet.

"Bristol," Beau said, addressing her. "I thought I came here to vet you, to make sure you and your family were safe for my sister to meet. But that's not why I was really here. I realize now that I came to Hope Falls to fall hopelessly in love with you. I was meant for you, and Hope brought us together."

The crowd awh-ed, and Bristol felt her cheeks flush. She blinked furiously, refusing to cry in front of the entire town. "Now, I screwed up," he told the crowd. "And Bristol graciously, grudgingly agreed to give me a second chance. Bristol, I hope tonight will make you proud of that decision."

She heard a hoot from the crowd and guessed it came from Tessa Maguire's direction.

Beau turned the microphone over to Alli and stepped back with Bristol. He kept her hand in his and squeezed it reassuringly.

"What's going on, Beau?" she whispered without moving her lips.

"Just know that we all love you, and this is the best way we could think of to say that."

Alli adjusted the microphone, and Beau squeezed Bristol's hand reassuringly. She could feel the energy of the crowd. Whatever this was, it was big enough that the entire town was anticipating what came next.

"My name is Alli, and I'm eighteen. I was a soccer player and honor student until I got sick. Last Christmas, my doctors told me that it would be my last one unless a miracle happened. And then one did. The Quinns decided to donate Hope's organs," she read from index cards. "I got Hope's heart." Her voice broke. Mary let go of her husband's hand and crossed to Alli, putting an arm around the girl's shoulder and squeezing. Alli grinned at her through tears. "You were my miracle. Hope saved my life. But I wasn't the only one."

Bristol's gaze flew to Beau's face. *He couldn't have. There was no way.*

"We were able to track down all of Hope's recipients, and they were all willing to give up their Christmas Eve plans to be here tonight."

Bristol didn't even have time to prepare. The tears turned on like a faucet. She was shaking her head, hiding her face in her hands.

"Hope Falls, please welcome Chester Upchurch." A man in his late fifties and a ridiculous Christmas sweater climbed the stairs of the bandstand. "He got Hope's corneas, and with his sight restored, he got to see his first grandson when he was born this summer."

Chester paused at each Quinn to hug them and whisper a few words to them. "It's a pleasure to meet you, Bristol," he whispered. "I can't thank you enough for changing my life."

Bristol was too choked up to speak. So she kissed him on the cheek. He waved to a group in the crowd, and someone held up a baby.

"Whitney Thrale is a mother of three, and with Hope's kidney, she was able to get off dialysis and start coaching soccer." A woman with miles of curly hair and tears in her eyes took the stage blowing the crowd and her family kisses. She kissed and thanked every member of the Quinn clan one at a time.

"Victor Urey was given less than forty-eight hours to live

when his family received word that a new liver with his name on it was being airlifted to Dallas. He and his wife, June, celebrated fifty years of marriage last month with a cruise to Hawaii," Alli continued.

Bristol couldn't see anymore. She was blinded by tears, the entire town of Hope Falls with her. They were all her family, and so were the people who now carried pieces of Hope.

They met eleven recipients, eleven friends, eleven new family members and their families. Bristol watched her parents rejoice in the beauty of the moment. Grandchildren met, daughters walked down aisles, colleges graduated. Their daughter, their beautiful Hope, had given hope to so many other families.

When it was over, when the high school chorus took the stage for their traditional Christmas concert, Beau swept Bristol up in his arms.

"Merry Christmas, Bristol."

"I love you, Beau. Thank you for this. Thank you from all of us..." she couldn't go on. There were tears in her eyes and a lump in her throat.

"I'd do anything for you, for your family."

"Our family," she corrected him. "It's all ours now. No backing out."

"You just made all my wishes come true," he said as he tenderly cupped her face.

"Well, not all of them. Not yet. This makes me glad I went overboard for your Christmas present."

"You *are* my Christmas present," he said squeezing her tight again.

"I'm not your only Christmas present. Alli helped me pick this one out."

"What did you do?"

"My turn now," Bristol winked. "Turn around."

As he did, she had the pleasure of seeing wonder and delight wash over his face as he took it all in. The Chicago Wind all dressed as Santa and all grinning from ear to ear waited in front of the Christmas tree.

"What? How?"

"Go say hi to your family," she said, giving him a push forward.

They met him halfway and tackled him to the ground as she'd seen them do in countless highlight reels.

"Damn, that was one hell of an idea," Alli announced at her side.

"I can't believe you got them all here," Bristol said, wiping more tears from her eyes. "And got them all dressed as Santa."

"Those guys would do anything for Beau. They have to turn around and fly back out tonight, but I think they'll all say this is worth it."

Alli abandoned her to join the fray where she was immediately welcomed, and Savannah appeared at Bristol's side. "You're making my Christmas gift to Vince look like crap," she announced.

"What did you get him?"

"Shirts with his initials monogrammed on the cuffs."

Bristol laughed and wrapped her arm around her sister. "He's an accountant. He'll love it."

Beau emerged from the manly love fest a few minutes later and dragged Bristol around introducing her to his teammates. She felt it in the air, the love that one girl had sparked.

"Thank you, Hope," she whispered. She held her breath when an icy blue orb shot up into the sky and a lone snowflake exploded into being in tones of blue and silver.

"Did you do this, Beau?"

"Shh, keep watching," he urged. So she did as a blizzard of snowflake fireworks lit up the night sky. The crowd oohed and ahhed as silver sparkles shimmered against the black. They painted the sky in a spectacular show, each one better than the last.

The finale began, dozens of fireworks exploding and glittering, raining light down over the town, until finally one spark shot skyward. Up, up, up it climbed, all eyes on it in anticipation, and when the silver heart bloomed open, Bristol felt the tears on her cheeks.

She looked to Beau again, but he wasn't standing next to her. He was kneeling, his green eyes damp and hopeful.

"Bristol, Alli has Hope's heart, and now I'm asking for yours. I owe you my life and my family. I came here to thank you, and here I am asking you for even more than you've already given me. I know it's too soon and too fast. But I want you every day of my life. I want Violet. I want Hope Falls. I want it all. Will you do me the great honor of being my wife, my partner, my center?"

The ring he held between gloved fingers sparkled brighter than all the fireworks in the sky.

Bristol cupped her hands to her cheeks, a sob of beautiful, exquisite joy escaping her lungs. And for that moment, she felt Hope with her, felt the nudge at her back, and knew without a doubt her sister's love lived on.

What are you waiting for? Hope wanted to know. *Jump, and he'll catch you.*

She couldn't speak, couldn't form the yes that her heart was shouting. But she could nod through her tears. Beau drew off her glove and reverently slipped the ring onto her finger, kissing it once before rising.

"I promise you, Bristol, I will never stop being grateful to you, and I will never forget your sister. Not just for saving my sister but giving me you. It wasn't fate that brought us together. It was Hope."

She jumped into his arms, and he picked her up off her feet and whirled her around. The crowd was cheering, and she didn't know if it was for them, for the fireworks, or for the memory of Hope.

"I love you, Beau, with all my heart.

BONUS EPILOGUE
CHAPTER ONE

Ten Years Later...

"Care to do the honors, Mrs. Evanko?" Beau, her handsome husband of nearly ten years handed Bristol the extension cord.

"I'd be honored to do the honors," Bristol said, stamping her feet on the porch floor boards to keep warm. "Drumroll, my handsome helper."

Beau obliged, drumming on the railing that he'd carved their initials into in a romantic, and splintery, gesture when they'd built the cabin.

"Let the Evanko-Quinn Christmas begin," Bristol announced, plugging the cord into the outlet. She pumped her fist into the air as the twelve-foot, snow-tipped pine lit up with a dozen strands of Christmas lights. "Yes! We didn't accidentally string up any of the blinky lights this time."

Beau draped an arm around her and pulled her into his side so they could admire their work.

Pretty as a picture. The snow was falling steadier now, adding to the already pristine blanket. Night would fall soon, and with it, would come the Quinns bearing side dishes and desserts and presents.

"You know, if that tree gets any bigger, we're going to need a bucket truck to decorate it," he mused.

"How about we just make the kids do it while we stay inside and drink hot chocolate?"

"I like where your head's at, gorgeous," Beau said, smiling down at her. "Especially if hot chocolate is a euphemism."

And suddenly the Sierra Nevada Christmas cold wasn't a factor anymore. Bristol still loved looking at him after ten years, kids, and more milestones than she could mark. Sure, the crinkles by his eyes were deeper, and there were more gray strands in his reddish-brown beard. But Beau only got better with age.

She looped her arms around his neck and stepped her boots between his. "Thanks for the last decade, Beau."

He gently stroked the long hair that spilled out from under her wool cap. "You're still happy after all this time?" he teased.

She nodded. "Deliriously."

"Good. Then I'm doing my job."

Bristol raised on tip toe and placed a soft kiss against his mouth. "I love you. Thanks for doing this for my family."

"Bristol, you say that every Christmas." That was her Beau, sweetly exasperated every time she felt the need to say thank you. It was because he was intent on spending *his* life thanking her.

"It means the world to all of us that we can be together here." She stretched her arm out to encompass the cabin. "Cabin" was an understatement. It was like calling a six-foot-seven professional hockey player "Tiny."

When Beau had announced that they were building a cabin six years ago, Bristol imagined a cozy little cottage with a stone fireplace. Well, she'd gotten the stone fireplace. All two-stories of it. And five bedrooms—plus a bunk room—and more bathrooms than she cared to clean. Also a kitchen fit for a gourmet chef and his or her extended family. Every year since its completion, they'd hosted Christmas. The more the merrier.

She took another breath of the crisp winter air. "I'm going to go inside and make sure the kids haven't fed the dog all of the Christmas cookies."

Beau pulled her in for a hard hug, pressing her face against the flannel jacket he wore. He smelled of sawdust and snow and pine, a heady combination.

"I'm going to do another pass on the driveway before everyone gets here."

"You just want to play with your new ATV," she teased, pulling back to look up at him.

He grinned boyishly, and her heart fluttered the way it always did when she spotted that dimple.

"I'll see you inside."

He gave her a quick kiss on the forehead and bounded down the porch steps.

Bristol paused at the front door as was her habit and ran her fingers over the angel and heart carving that Beau had commissioned for the house.

Hope lives here.

Bristol stepped inside the front door shaking snow off her hat and vest.

"Mom!" The call came in surround sound as both Violet and Aaron vied for her attention from opposite ends of the great room.

"One at a time," Bristol laughed. "Is anyone bleeding?"

"No," they groaned in unison.

"I started the fire in the fireplace just like Dad showed me," eight-year-old Aaron announced proudly from the living room. He looked so much like a miniature version of his father —taller than nearly every kid in his class, shaggy auburn hair, and those sea green eyes. It had been a shock to them both that, personality-wise, he'd taken after the Aunt Hope he'd never meet.

"I can't find the pecans," Violet called from the kitchen. At eighteen, she was as tall as her mother and, in Bristol's humble opinion, a beautiful, kind soul... as long as you didn't try to wake her before ten.

Bristol paused in front of the fireplace to admire Aaron's handiwork and kissed him on top of the head. "It's perfect, bud. When you're done here, do you want to sneak the gift bags into everyone's rooms?"

His green eyes lit up. "Yes!"

It was another Evanko tradition. On Christmas Eve, they welcomed their guests with little gift bags of cookies and goodies and silly trinkets. Everyone's favorite part of the gift bag was the name of the Angel Tree child that Bristol and Beau and the kids had shopped for and the list of gifts they'd purchased in their honor.

Aaron hastily cleaned up the newspaper and kindling that he'd strewn about the hearth and made the mad dash for Beau and Bristol's bedroom.

"Just the gift bags, Aaron. Leave the wrapped ones alone," Bristol called after him.

"What time is Aunt Alli coming?" Violet asked.

Bristol joined her daughter in the kitchen, giving her tomboy daughter's ponytail a tug as she looked over her shoulder.

"That looks beautiful, Vi," she said peering at the pecan

pie her daughter was making. Another sweet reminder of Hope. "Aunt Alli and Uncle Samaar will be here by dinner."

"They should know whether they're having a boy or a girl by now," Violet said, weaving two pieces of pie dough into a fancy crust. It was her daughter's creative expression on an old family tradition. As was the letter H over a cutout heart baked in the center of the pie. Just looking at it made Bristol a little misty, missing her sister and wondering what Hope would think of their lives now.

"Maybe they don't want to find out what they're having," Bristol pointed out.

"I think it's a girl," Violet announced, putting the pie on a baking sheet and sliding it into the oven.

"Definitely a boy," Aaron countered as he raced through the kitchen with gift bags looped over both arms.

"She!"

"He!"

"As long as the baby is—"

"Healthy," Vi and Aaron announced with twin eyerolls.

"We know, Mom," Violet said, hip-checking Bristol to take the sting out of her rebuke.

Health was always a concern. Eleven years ago, Beau's little sister had lived what was supposed to be her last Christmas. But in a cruel and beautiful twist of fate, Bristol's sister had died instead. Hope's heart had saved Alli's life. And now, more than a decade later, Alli the half-marathon runner, spinach smoothie-drinker, and marketing executive for the American Transplant Foundation, was four months pregnant.

The entire family was thrilled.

"Mom!" Aaron poked his head over the railing of the upstairs loft wielding two gift bags. "Who are these two for? They don't have names."

"Oh, those are extras," Bristol lied. "Just put them in the back bedroom, okay?"

"'Kay!" he yelled.

Violet smirked at the thunder of her little brother's feet above.

BONUS EPILOGUE

CHAPTER TWO

The ham was in the oven. The potatoes were boiling. The bottles of wine were open. The tree and candles were lit. And nearly all of their guests had arrived. Nolan, Bristol's ex-husband and father to Violet, and his Halle Berry-lookalike wife, Lissa, had just arrived with their two kids, Lyric and Dexter. While they unpacked their SUV load of gifts and luggage and kid accessories, the rest of the crew including Bristol's parents and her older sister's family were crowded around the big leather ottoman in the living room playing a game and laughing.

Bristol watched them from the bottom of the staircase and felt her heart fill with blessings. Beau was missing from the chaos, and she spotted him in the foyer examining the Christmas cards they hung on the wall. There were dozens of them. Her favorites weren't the ones from Beau's old PHL teammates. And they weren't all of the family and friend cards either. Her very favorites, the ones she always hung in the middle, were the ten that came from the other people whose lives Hope had saved.

Bristol wrapped an arm around Beau's waist. "Doing a little light reading?" she asked, pressing a kiss to his cheek.

"Just feeling beyond lucky," he said.

"Me, too," Bristol whispered.

They both heard the engine of a car, and Beau squeezed her shoulder. "Alli and Samaar are here," he called to the living room. A cheer erupted.

Beau and Bristol stepped out onto the front porch and watched as the couple climbed out of their SUV. Alli's little rounded belly was barely visible under her turtleneck, but just the glimpse of it was enough to send a bolt of joy through Bristol's heart.

Beau jogged down the steps and swept his sister up into a hug that brought her feet out of the snow. "Missed you, Al."

Samaar, ever fashionable in a cranberry cashmere scarf, grabbed Bristol for a tight hug. "How's my favorite sis-in-law?" he asked, giving her an extra squeeze.

"Great. How was your drive?" she asked.

"Long!" Alli winked, playfully shoving her husband out of the way so she could hug Bristol. "Don't hug me too hard because I have to pee."

Bristol laughed. "Well, then. Let's get you inside to some indoor plumbing."

They did just that, and after another round of hugs and greetings and one bathroom break, they all sprawled out on the couches and chairs in the living room.

The chatter of a dozen conversations rose over the crackling of the fire and the snoring of Savannah's dog, Honey.

Bristol saw Samaar and Alli share a secret smile, and then Samaar brought the whistle to his lips.

Another tradition, Beau's coaching whistle had been commandeered one Christmas when Nana Ludavine couldn't get the family to shut up for four seconds. Since then, it had become part and parcel of nearly every Evanko-Quinn get-together.

They moved to stand in front of the Christmas tree, facing the rest of them. Samaar nervously twirled the whistle on his finger.

"What's going on?" Big Bob Quinn, Bristol's dad asked.

"Yeah, you two look suspicious," Savannah, Bristol's older sister observed.

"We wanted to wait to do this until everyone was together," Alli announced.

Beau pulled Bristol into his lap where he sprawled on the leather armchair. "Baby news?" he whispered in her ear, his voice hopeful.

"Last week we..." Alli cleared her throat, and her eyes clouded with tears.

Oh, God. Bristol froze. *Was it bad news?*

Samaar rubbed Alli's back. "What my wife is trying to say and can't get out, due to pregnancy hormones and general holiday mushiness, is that we found out what we're having last week." He grinned. Alli was glowing too despite the silent tears.

Bristol sagged with relief against Beau. He stroked her thigh through her jeans.

"Anyway, we know that all we're supposed to want is a healthy baby. But we both were *hoping* for..." He paused and gazed down at Alli. She was smiling and crying and shining so brightly that Bristol could feel the joy radiating off of her.

"A girl. We were hoping for a girl, and we're having one," Alli blurted out.

Mary, Bristol's mother, squealed in delight, jumping up and clapping her hands. "A baby girl! We're having a baby girl!"

Aaron slouched onto the couch next to six-year-old Dexter. "Another girl. Great."

"A baby girl named Hope," Alli added.

Squeals turned to gasps and then tears.

"For the love of God, will someone get me some tissues," Savannah wailed from the couch. Vince, her husband in a hideous reindeer sweater, scrambled for the box on the end table, his own eyes misty.

"A baby girl named Hope," Mary sniffled. "We get another Hope."

Violet was crying softly as Aaron helpfully shoved the tissues in her direction.

Bob mopped at his own eyes with his sleeves.

Nolan's wife Lissa tearfully grabbed Lyric in a headlock and squeezed her daughter tight.

"Mom! You're crushing me." Lyric's arms flailed, and Nolan did his best to pry his wife off her.

Bristol pressed her face into Beau's chest and squeezed him tight before jumping out of his lap. She crossed the living room and wrapped Alli in a hug. They swayed side to side for a long, quiet moment. Tears, salty and sweet, decorated their cheeks.

"I want in on this!" Mary elbowed her way into the hug. "Grammy wants a hug!"

Savannah and Lissa weren't about to be left out. The women joined in, wrapping their arms around everyone.

"Hey, I helped make this baby," Samaar pointed out from outside their tight, tearful circle.

"Get in here." Bristol pulled him into the center.

"Group hug," Violet announced. And everyone joined them in front of the tree, a tangle of arms, a flood of tears, a shared joy so palpable they could all feel it.

"I told you they'd like it," Alli sniffled at Samaar.

"Are you sure they like it? They're all crying. I think they hate the idea," he joked.

"Shut up, Samaar!" They shouted as one.

Christmas Eve dinner was its usual chaotic, two-hour party. Too much wine, too many cookies, and plenty of laughter. They dined by candlelight in their pajamas, all talking at once. The dining room table, a fourteen-foot behemoth, had room for everyone. And just like every other year, Bristol held Beau's hand under the table.

They had plenty to be grateful for every holiday season. Beau had retired from the PHL before they met. But he'd been smart and careful with his money. They'd invested in real estate and a few commercial ventures, freeing him up to dabble in the hardware store and apartments next-door, while still lending a hand over at Bristol's Early Bird Café. The café's business was brisk and profitable. She'd paid back the money her parents and Nolan—God bless him for being the best ex-husband and co-parent a woman could want—had lent her.

She no longer woke in cold sweats wondering how she'd send Vi to college. And college was right around the corner for her high school senior. Her terror-on-skates high school senior. Thanks to Beau and Violet's combined influence, the high school started a women's ice hockey team, coached by none other than the legendary PHL hero Beau Evanko.

He'd fit seamlessly into her family, becoming a second dad to Violet and giving Bristol another sister in Alli. He'd been welcomed by her parents and her hard-ass divorce attorney sister. Even her crazy Italian aunts and Nana Ludavine loved him. They'd all be here tomorrow for Christmas brunch. The men would retire to the basement with its big screen TV and line of recliners when the women got too loud and wild on the main floor.

Traditions. No matter how much a family changed, there were traditions to uphold.

And things would be just a little louder, a little wilder next year with baby Hope. Bristol savored a sip of wine only half-listening to the laughter and conversations around the table.

Beau tossed something small and shiny at Violet. Ever the athlete, she caught it one handed. Beau gave her a subtle nod. She grinned at him and blew a sharp trill from the whistle.

Honey whimpered and ran out from under the table where she'd lurked in search of handouts.

Conversation came to a screeching halt.

"I have some news," Violet announced.

Bristol frowned at Beau. *How did her daughter have news that she wasn't aware of?*

Violet took a deep breath.

"Well, spit it out already," Aaron encouraged.

"Give them the shirts, Beau," Violet said in a stage whisper.

On cue, Beau reached under the table producing several rolled up t-shirts. He handed one to Bristol and winked.

Bristol unfurled the shirt and held it up.

UW Badger Mom

A pair of hockey sticks crossed in an X under the words.

"No. *Way.*"

Violet nodded vehemently. "Yes way. I got into University of Wisconsin," she said in a rush. "I'm going to be a Badger!"

Bristol let out a "whoop" and slapped the table with her palm in excitement. Her baby girl was going to her dream college, her first choice. Not that Bristol was by any means ready to let Violet go. But she had a few months to work her way up to it.

"That's not all," Beau's deep voice broke through excited congratulations.

"I also made the team... and got a partial scholarship," Violet grinned.

Bristol stood up so fast she knocked her chair over. She raced around the table, grabbing Violet from behind for a hug. Nolan rose to join the embrace.

"I'm so damn proud of you, kiddo," he whispered.

Bristol would have echoed the sentiment, but the lump in her throat was preventing any words from getting out. She pressed a kiss to Violet's head and met Beau's gaze. He was glowing with pride. Violet was as much his as she was Nolan's, and they were all more than okay with that.

She released Violet and returned to her husband. "You sneak," she hissed poking him in the shoulder.

He pushed his chair back and pulled her into his lap. "I just happened to be there when she got the email and ran to find out why she was screaming."

"This is just the best Christmas Eve ever," Mary proclaimed. Bob was too busy proudly pulling on his UW Badger Grandpa t-shirt over his pajama top.

"I don't think I can take any more surprises tonight," Savannah said. "If there are any more, can we please hold them until tomorrow?"

The doorbell rang, and the table quieted.

"Who would be showing up here on Christmas Eve?" Beau wondered. "Are the aunts coming early?"

"Why don't you go find out," Bristol suggested. "And maybe take Alli with you?"

"What are you up to, gorgeous?" he demanded, rising from his chair.

Bristol smiled innocently. "I have no idea what you're talking about. Hurry up."

Beau and Alli made their way to the front door.

"*Mom? Dad?*" Alli's shocked announcement sent a ripple of gasps down the table.

"Hey, Mom, you want to go grab two more plates from the kitchen?" Bristol suggested. She took her wine into the foyer where Alli was hugging their mother and Beau was gaping at their father as if he were the ghost of Christmas past.

"Bristol!" Gladys Evanko reached for her daughter-in-law.

"You did this?" Alli asked in shock as her mother and Bristol embraced.

Bristol had invited the Evankos to every Christmas celebration. But their work, leading relief efforts in various parts of the world, always came first. This year, Bristol wasn't willing to take no for an answer. It had been three long years since they'd last visited. That visit, though short, had gone a long way in repairing the rift between parents and the children who had been set aside for a greater good.

Beau shook his father's hand and pulled Don in for a one-armed hug. "It's good to see you, Dad."

"Oh, my! Our little girl is having a baby," Gladys sighed, admiring her daughter's tiny belly.

"Your little girl is having a little girl," Alli said, patting her stomach.

"What smells so good in here?" Don asked, rubbing his hands together on the way to the dining room.

BONUS EPILOGUE
CHAPTER THREE

Bristol stepped out of the bathroom and into the bedroom to find Beau sprawled naked across the flannel quilt. He hadn't been a professional athlete in over a decade, but he'd certainly held on to the physique.

The electric candles in the bay window bathed the room in a soft glow. Outside the snow fell steadily, quietly, beckoning her.

Bristol crossed to the window and stared out at the midnight Christmas scene. The lights on the pine shone from under a new layer of snow on the branches. In the distance, the Sierras glowed white against the inky purple sky.

It was picture perfect. And everything felt right.

She felt Beau behind her, and then he was wrapping his arms around her. Those big, capable hands that had changed her life, traveling her body on a never-ending exploration.

Bristol leaned her head back against his broad shoulder.

"Beautiful night," she whispered, twining her arms around him over her head.

He skimmed his palms over her breasts. Her nipples tightened in reaction to the heat of his hands and the silk of her nightshirt. Beau gave a rumble of approval deep in his chest. "It might be a beautiful night, but there is nothing more beautiful in this world to me than you, Bristol."

"Beau," she sighed out his name with love, with want.

He slid his hands down her waist, over her hips, until his busy fingers found the hem of her nightshirt. With the whisper of silk, he pulled the shirt up and over her head, discarding it on the plush, ivory rug.

"That's better," he murmured against her throat. His hands continued their lazy tour of her body.

He was hard for her, achingly so. Seeing him wanting her never failed to ignite her own desire. Even after so many years together, babies, and weddings, and now college. It was a life better than Bristol could have ever dreamed for herself.

"I love you, Beau," she whispered into the snowy night.

He pressed her forward with his weight against her back. And Bristol braced herself against the window, palms on the cold glass.

With the patience of a man who knew what good was yet to come, Beau pushed into her slick center. He took his time, moving, worshipping, loving.

Bristol trembled beneath his touch as she had a thousand times before. No one knew her body better.

Those capable hands returned to her breasts to squeeze and tug and stroke. She could feel the heat of his breath, the rough of his beard, against her bare shoulder.

This was love. And this. And this.

They moved together to music only they could hear, reverently chasing each other toward the peak.

Her breath, short and hot, fogged the glass until all that was left was candlelight and Beau.

"My love. My life," Beau chanted the words softly and Bristol felt him go impossibly harder inside her.

He released one breast and brought his hand to the apex of her thighs. She let out a quiet little moan when he used his fingers on her. Stroking her inside and out, he carried her to the light.

"Beau. Yes. Yes. Yes." Her words were a breathy gasp as the orgasm built, rising like the sun over the mountains. She gave herself over to the rapture of the glow that spread throughout her body.

He stiffened against her and groaned as he came. He poured himself into her, his love, his seed. And as she had a thousand times before, Bristol whispered a silent thank you.

Eventually, they found the bed, sliding between the soft flannel sheets and pulling the quilt up around them. They rarely used the fireplace in the bedroom. Though winters in the Sierras were cold, Beau put off more than enough heat for them both.

Bristol curled against his side, resting her cheek on his chest where she could listen to the steady thrum of his heart.

She traced her fingers over the tattoo there.

Hope.

A few years ago, after a few beers and no kids at home for the night, they'd walked to a tattoo parlor on a whim. It was Beau's idea and had only cemented the love she had for him. The love she insisted couldn't get any deeper and daily, *daily,* it did. She felt rooted and strong with Beau by her side. And none of this would be possible if it weren't for her sister.

Beau ran his finger over her matching tattoo, small and dainty on the inside of her bicep. A daily reminder of the woman who couldn't physically be here with them but still made her presence known in beautiful and unexpected ways.

"I have to ask. How did you get my parents in the country, much less our part of it?" Beau asked.

Bristol laughed softly. "It took about two months of convincing. I started in June and came up with a solution to every excuse. By the way, you and I may have to travel to Haiti next spring to do some building."

Beau chuckled and ran his hand down her arm. The touch warmed her and sent a zing through her blood. She let her hand wander across his chest, down his taut abs. She watched in hazy delight as he hardened again at her touch.

"You are a biological miracle," she teased.

"*That* is a guarantee, my beautiful and ever-so-sexy wife. But first, Santa brought you something else."

He held up a small black box.

"Beau," Bristol sighed. "You always go overboard!"

"I have everything I've ever wanted, and all of my favorite people are under one roof on the most magical night of the year. Of course I'm going to mark the occasion."

Spoiled was an excellent adjective for how Beau made her feel three hundred and sixty-five days a year.

Bristol held the box aloft and opened it.

"Oh, my god, Beau," she breathed.

He took the box from her and freed the necklace. It was a large diamond heart that glittered like the snow falling outside their window on a long, gold chain.

"I got you a long chain so you can wear it to work under your clothes without worrying about it catching on anything," he said, looping it over her head and adjusting the diamond where it fell between her breasts.

"It's stunning," Bristol whispered.

"So are you," he insisted.

"Damn it, Beau! I really wanted to win the present war this year!"

"Gorgeous, neither one of us is ever going to win the present war. Someone else already did."

"Who?" Bristol asked, holding up the diamond to admire it in the candlelight.

"Hope," he said. "She saved my sister, and she brought me you."

AUTHOR'S NOTE TO THE READER

Dear Reader,

Thank you so much for reading Beau and Bristol's story! I cried every damn day writing this book and when Mr. Lucy read it, he announced, "If this doesn't make you feel something, you're dead inside."

Actually, he had to spell it out for me because when he first came into my office and pointed at his eyes I thought he was telling me he was getting pink eye. I didn't realize that my story had moved him to a sheen of eye moisture. Once we cleared that up—the misunderstanding, not the imaginary pink eye—I celebrated knowing that at least it wasn't just me camping out in the feels department.

Anyway, here are a few things you might not have known about this book:

1.   Bristol, Savannah, and Hope were all named after the places they were conceived, which the girls thought was disgusting so they never discuss it.

2.   This story was inspired by a viral video of the bride

who invited her father's heart recipient to walk her down the aisle. I ugly cried. It was amazing.

3.   Bristol and Beau's story was supposed to be an adorable, petite novella. I appear to be incapable of writing anything under 50,000 words. So you got yourself a short, chubby novel here.

If you liked this small town romance, check out my Blue Moon Series set in the cozy upstate New York home of nosy hippie matchmakers. If you totally fell in love with this story or just me, sign up for my newsletter and follow me on Facebook. I have a crazy great reader group on Facebook, too. Come visit! And if you want more from Hope Falls, check out Melanie Shawn's series on Amazon.

Thanks for reading! Don't stop!

Xoxo,
Lucy

ABOUT THE AUTHOR

Lucy Score is a *Wall Street Journal* and #1 Amazon bestselling author. She grew up in a literary family who insisted that the dinner table was for reading and earned a degree in journalism. She writes full-time from the Pennsylvania home she and Mr. Lucy share with their obnoxious cat, Cleo. When not spending hours crafting heartbreaker heroes and kick-ass heroines, Lucy can be found on the couch, in the kitchen, or at the gym. She hopes to someday write from a sailboat, or oceanfront condo, or tropical island with reliable Wi-Fi.

Sign up for her newsletter and stay up on all the latest Lucy book news.
And follow her on:
Website: Lucyscore.com
Facebook at: lucyscorewrites
Instagram at: scorelucy
Readers Group at: Lucy Score's Binge Readers Anonymous

ACKNOWLEDGMENTS

Thank you so much to the writing duo Melanie Shawn for inviting me to be part of the Hope Falls family. I enjoyed my visit to your world!

As always, my books would be total crap without the eagle eyes of Dawn, my amazing proofer, and Amanda, my lovely line editor. Thanks, ladies!

Kari March Designs for the fabulous cover.

Special thanks to Mr. Lucy for being ever ready with the tissues when I cried my way through this book.

And last but never, ever least, thank you to my readers. You are the reason I put on my writing pants every day. Well, more like writing leggings. Same thing and I'll fight anyone who disagrees.

LUCY'S TITLES

Standalone Titles

Undercover Love

Pretend You're Mine

Finally Mine

Protecting What's Mine

Mr. Fixer Upper

The Christmas Fix

Heart of Hope

The Worst Best Man

Rock Bottom Girl

The Price of Scandal

By a Thread

Forever Never

Things We Never Got Over

Riley Thorn

Riley Thorn and the Dead Guy Next Door

Riley Thorn and the Corpse in the Closet

Riley Thorn and the Blast from the Past

The Blue Moon Small Town Romance Series

No More Secrets

Fall into Temptation

The Last Second Chance

Not Part of the Plan

Made in United States
Orlando, FL
05 April 2024

45472231R00139